BRUTAL BEAST

VICIOUS VIPERS MC 5

LYNN BURKE

BRUTAL BEAST

I'm a no-filter, use fists first kind of man who's suspicious of everyone and everything. As the president of the Vicious Vipers MC, it's my duty to protect my brothers, and I take pleasure in doing so.

When a sassy woman who heats my blood moves in next door, I tell myself I don't want the baggage she brings, even if he is a respectful kid who weasels his way into my heart. She's jaded. A stubborn, lying wildcat I can't resist, and I'm determined to find the truth of her identity and claim her.

But I've got secrets of my own, long buried in the woods of Maine, that unearthed would define me as the brutal beast she fears me to be.

She's mine to protect—even if my sins are brought to light, destroying any hope for our future.

DEDICATION

For my lovie, Lidia

CONTENTS

1

———

VIGIL

My cell vibrated in my back pocket, and I cut the mower's engine and swiped at the sweat running down my face before fishing it out. I grunted at the club whore's name on the screen.

"Yeah?"

"Vigil!" Tina's voice caught on a sob, and I scowled deeper at her unusual display of emotion. "Ricky and Bucky got into it—they're still at it!"

A loud crash sounded in the background, and she shrieked.

"What the fuck?" I muttered.

"You need to get down here!" Tina said, hysteria rising in her voice. "Bucky's gonna kill him!"

Shit. "Did you call Ryker?" My Sergeant at Arms

worked at the chop shop at the back of the compound.

"He hasn't come in yet!"

"Be right there." Scowling, I hung up and left my mower in the half-cut backyard. Stalking into my house for a shirt and my bike keys, I muttered more than my fair share of curses.

My younger brother had been in a majorly fucked-up funk lately. Moody and volatile to the point he'd broken a few noses and blackened eyes when provoked. I'd laid him out flat twice in the previous couple of months, but he refused to talk about what had shoved so far up his ass he'd turned into a little bitch.

He'd taken to drinking the hard shit and a lot of it. His ass had been drunk more often than not. I'd been thinking he needed a good talking to, threats and shit. Guess it was time.

A fucking Monday, ten in the morning, and he'd already gotten into it. Bucky might be a smaller guy, but he was wiry and scrappy as fuck. Ricky had barked up the wrong damn tree.

My Harley roared to life between my thighs, and I took off out of my neighborhood, the wind on my face a welcome respite from the damn August heatwave gripping New England. It took all of five minutes to get to the club, but the sweat still hadn't dried by the time I got there. The gate to the Vicious Vipers MC began rolling back when I rounded the bend, and I had to slow before weaseling my way through the old thing without acknowledging whoever manned the guard house.

The club's door stood open, my jackass brother stumbled through it into the sun, Bucky holding him in a headlock. Still fucking at it, the stupid fucks.

Still scowling, I parked my bike and kicked down the stand, the sounds of Ricky's fists on Bucky's stomach, their grunts and curses filled the air.

Tina appeared in the doorway, her eyes wild, mascara streaks down her pale cheeks.

Temptation to let the two men work their shit out warred over preservation of life. Just in case things did get ugly, though, I decided to step in.

I grasped Bucky's hair and yanked him away from my brother.

Bucky jerked backward with a swing, but I side stepped and grabbed Ricky as he went to charge the smaller man.

"Enough!" I barked again, my gaze flitting between the two men. "Just calm your goddamn britches, boys!"

Bucky finally focused on my face—and went still as fuck, hands fisted at his sides, chest heaving. He sported a cut on his lip and the beginnings of a shiner he'd have to brag about in the coming week.

"Vigil." He at least acknowledged me.

Ricky spit blood and yanked free of me, his wild hair glinting more red than auburn in the sun. The fucker could have been my twin, but we couldn't have been more different.

"The fuck is going on?" I looked between the two as they took their battle to a stare-down.

Movement in my periphery caught my attention. Ryker sauntered out of the club, two bottles of water in his hands. He tossed one to both Ricky and Bucky, his forehead furrowed as deep as mine.

"The fuck is going on?" I asked again.

Ricky's lips remained clamped, and he swayed on his feet.

"Are you drunk?" I asked, my frown deepening.

"Yeah," Bucky answered for him. "Caught his ass stealing a bottle of JD from behind the bar."

"I told you to supply your own shit," I said, turning back toward my brother.

"Ran out," he snipped.

"Then you're done until you sober up to drive to the damn liquor store! Goddamnit, Ricky." My hand itched to cuff him upside the head, but I expected that would start another brawl, one he definitely wouldn't win in his fucked up condition. "I've had about enough of your shit. You need to sober up for good. If you can't do it on your own, get your ass in rehab. I'm done, Ricky. Seriously. Make a change or I'm taking your colors."

The air charged around us as Ricky stared at me, his pale eyes so like my own, void of emotion. "You'd do that?" he slurred.

"Damn right, I will. Should have given you that ultimatum weeks ago."

He turned and staggered toward the club's entrance, and Tina stepped aside to let him pass. She hugged herself, her face still pale.

"How bad is it in there?" I asked, nodding toward the interior.

"Bad."

I nodded to Bucky. "Get your ass back in there and start to clean up."

"What about Ricky?" he muttered like a petulant brat, the little shit.

"Just get your ass in there or you won't be *getting* your damn colors," I barked at the pledge, having had enough bullshit for the morning. Add in the fucking heat, and I toed the line of losing my shit.

He scurried away, and I stalked after him, Ryker falling in beside me.

"Where the hell were you?" I asked him.

"Talia is getting her first molars. Whining and crying. I was trying to help," he grumbled.

"Pia okay?" I asked about his wife of almost two years.

"She told me to leave."

"You must have been one miserable bastard if she told you to get the fuck out of the house," I muttered while stepping into the club.

"Fuck off. You've never had to deal with that shit."

"Never want to, either." Hands on my hips, I surveyed the damage and stretched my neck side to side.

A smashed table. Two broken chairs. The custom made dart board lay on the ground in two pieces, the VV rockers around the bullseye split with jagged edges. I wondered who'd gotten the wooden plank over the head and how Hammer and Crow would feel about their favorite pastime being unavailable until I could get it replaced.

Ricky and Bucky had been behind the bar, too. Glass and liquid lay fucking everywhere. The liquor fumes in the air damn near watered my eyes.

"Goddamnit." I huffed a pissed off sigh. "I gotta get him outta here, don't I?" I asked Ryker quietly as Bucky and Tina picked up pieces of broken glass and tossed them into a barrel.

He pulled up a chair to the closest table and sat. "If he won't open up and tell you what the fuck his problem is, maybe."

I slunk into the chair beside him. "I really don't want to take his colors."

"As VP, he should know better."

Scrubbing a hand down over my face, I eyed the destruction. I would have to call in Hammer and Crow to fix the dented drywall, broken table, and chairs. "Yeah, he should," I finally agreed.

We both had demons, but I'd always seemed to have a better grip on their reins. Ricky had become a ticking time bomb and I didn't know what the fuck to do about it.

"Maybe a change of scenery would be good for him."

I considered Ryker's words while Bucky grabbed a package of paper towels from the storage closet. "Talk to Klingon lately?" I asked, turning back toward Ryker.

He eyed the mess, too, his hazel-green eyes less cold and calculating since his old ass had claimed

Pia and he'd become a father. "Everything in Vegas has been quiet."

I nodded, happy to hear there'd been no change. We'd made one hell of a mess out there years earlier, ending a few lives to save Stone's woman, and our Viper brothers from the Vegas chapter had helped to clean it up.

"Jenny?" I asked after Ryker's sister who had moved out there not long after her and Ryker's mom passed.

"Doing pretty good. Klingon still checks up on her even though there's no need."

A subtle threat had concerned Ryker enough he'd asked his childhood friend who happened to be the Vegas chapter's president to keep an eye on her. But that threat had been eradicated when we'd helped put the Martínez cartel and the Russian mob in the New England area behind bars two years earlier.

We might be one-percenters who didn't hesitate to take life or make tens of thousands though our chop shop and extortion opportunities, but I didn't allow drugs or sex slaves. Fuck knew my childhood had enough of both.

My father had been addicted to the first, and in true battered woman syndrome, my mom was nothing more than the second to him.

I stood, the sudden need to move and erase memories from my mind kicking into gear. "Let's clean this fucking place up," I grumbled. "I'll decide what to do with my brother's ass later."

———

Took us most of the day to set things right, and I ended up staying for steaks Tina slapped on the grill out back as brothers began to show up after their nine-to-fives. Hammer and Crow fixed their precious dart board, thank fuck, and puffed on cigs while tossing them, frothing mugs in their other hands.

Bucky manned the bar along with Greed since the place jammed like it usually did after a long as fuck Monday. Some bullshit dance music played thanks to Stone's woman who sat on his lap in the chair beside me. Devil and Dasia sat on my other side, sucking face and ignoring reality as they'd been doing for two years since they'd found one another.

Sully, Sin, and a handful of others played cards at the table beside us, tossing back shots like water —but they could hold theirs.

Ricky didn't show, keeping to his small apart-ment above the club, hopefully still sleeping it off. I missed my sober brother and having him beside me, but found contentment with the peace we'd had as a club for a few years.

Devil had dug up some shit on one of our state's congress women and she paid a pretty penny to the anonymous blackmailer to keep the images of her using a strap-on on her personal assistant from her husband.

The chop shop had also done well the last couple of months, the black market hot for shit we'd gotten our hands on, and the mob and cartel goons still sat in cold cells. As a club, we'd been enjoying the good life to the point my neck tingled on occasion as I wondered what lay around the corner. It'd been quiet. Too quiet.

Dasia giggled as Devil grasped her hips and ground her against him. "Like that pussy cat?" he murmured, completely lost in her and not giving two shits that I sat less than a foot away from their dry humping.

Giada sat facing Stone, all googly-eyed in love, the soft smile on her face for him alone.

I shifted, thinking to ease the sudden strange ache in my chest. Wondering if my blood pressure was up, I rubbed over my pecs while scowling. Didn't hurt—at least, not physically. I knew I was a jealous fucker over my brothers' having found their old ladies, but that wouldn't cause chest pains, would it?

"Vigil?"

I turned back toward Giada to find her focus on me, her smile gone. "Hmm?"

"You okay?" She motioned toward my hand still rubbing at my chest.

"Yeah." I managed a half smirk, slapped my palm down onto the table calling it a night, pulling the attention of the other love birds around me. "Think I'm done for the day. Fucking beat."

"Not off to find a whore to suck your dick?" Giada asked with a laugh before she and Dasia made gagging noises.

What was it with the old ladies and making faces over my usual hand-slapping a table at night's end and the truth about what I usually went in search of?

"Too fucking tired," I muttered as they continued to snicker.

"It's been weeks since you've gone off looking to get your dick sucked. Starting to think you need some little blue pills."

I glared at Devil.

He held up his hands and leaned back in his

chair, but his smirk stayed in place, the pretty boy pansy-assed motherfucker.

"If I liked boys, I'd make *you* get on your knees for me," I shot back.

"The hell you would," Dasia said with a laugh. "I don't share."

Yeah, neither did I—and dicks other than my own didn't do jack shit for me.

I stood, clasped a few brothers' hands, and headed into the humid night, their ribbing following me out the damn door.

Ten minutes later, the ache in my chest lingered as I turned into my neighborhood, enjoying the leisurely ride unlike the one earlier in the morning. I approached Widow Betsy's old house and eyed it as I'd been doing every time I'd passed in the previous two weeks. Her son had decided to rent rather than sell after she'd passed, but I'd yet to see the people who'd moved in beyond their teenage son. He'd been out and about on a bike as though looking for friends—or trouble.

A curvy backside on the stoop caught my attention, but the woman straightened and slipped inside the front door without glancing my way even though she must have heard the Harley between my legs. I'd seen enough to stir my dick to life, though. Tall, wavy dark hair even though I preferred blondes, and a juicy ass to set my mouth to drooling.

Fuck. Me.

I'd gone too damn long without getting laid. Hadn't even let one of the club whores treat my dick like a lollipop in months, not just weeks like Devil had noted. I hadn't been interested—figured maybe my balls were on their way out even though I'd just crested the forty mark.

Neighbor lady brought on a chub, so guess I wasn't needing those blue pills just yet.

I drove around the block and pulled into my garage, my mind still on the woman I hadn't gotten a good enough look at and that fucking ass.

Was she single? I hadn't seen a man around, but I also wasn't interested in hooking up with a single mom. Last thing I needed was some teenage punk cock-blocking me from getting my dick wet.

At least she'd brought the fucker back to life. I could live with that.

I made a mental note to hit Devil up for info on the new renters—just in case the woman wanted my dick down her throat.

2

MILA

The house wasn't much to speak of considering what we'd left behind, but it would do for the two of us. At least the rental came fully furnished since we'd left everything back home —including our identities.

I peered at the new Massachusetts driver's license that had been provided, hating the dark hair and name that wasn't what I'd been given at birth. Michelle Evans. Who was she? A single mom new to town, a janitor at the small retirement community down the road.

A woman I didn't recognize.

Tossing the license back onto the table in our small kitchen, I glanced around, any sense of hope or dreams I'd had as a younger woman with her future ahead of her smothered like burning flames from a bucket of cold water.

There was no ignoring the *how* we'd ended up in New England, far from where I'd been born and raised my own son, but the why questions still rang between my ears.

Why had I thought he would be a good dad for my boy?

Why hadn't I paid attention to the red flags those first couple of months?

Why hadn't I left at the first evidence he truly was a demon?

Blowing a heavy breath through my lips, I got up, and shoved the license back in my purse along with the credit card that also showed my fake name.

At least he wouldn't find me.

We could start over and live without fear. Devon, at fifteen, also had a different name and would start at a new high school in the fall. He would make new friends but would need to keep our lives on the west coast to himself. His longer blond locks had been buzzed clean off his head, changing his appearance as well.

My little boy no longer looked like one, and while he'd yet to fill out like a man, he sported the beginnings of scruff on his jawline and chin. At least he hadn't been plagued with acne like I had as a teenager.

The sounds of a mower came to life through the flimsy screen, drawing me to the kitchen's lone window above the sink that overlooked a small backyard. I leaned forward to better see the neighbor diagonally across from us, the rising sun starting to heat up the morning air again. The warming air caressed my face as I stared.

Shirtless. Muscles for miles, shoulders broad and strong. Tattoos. A near-ginger and full beard. Hot as hell from what I could make out.

He'd mowed about half of his backyard before taking off on a Harley the morning before. I'd been staring then, too, but once a motorcycle had roared to life and he drove out of his double garage, that same bucket of water smothered the heat that had flared to life inside me.

I'd had my fill of bikers. Especially ones that wore cuts like my semi-neighbor. I knew too well what rockers were, what they meant. He'd driven past late the night before, too, but I'd hurried inside, not even wanting to be neighborly and turn to wave.

Not checking him out covertly wasn't an option, though. The sight of him drew me in like hot, sandy beaches to California girls. A woman could dream, right? Fantasize, at least.

"Mom."

I spun from the window and smiled. "Yeah, baby?"

Devon sauntered into the kitchen, tossing a football into the air, the loss of dirty blond curls still catching me off guard. "Whatcha looking at?"

"Nothing." I turned to focus on the pile of breakfast dishes in the sink. "Are you excited to start school?"

"Nah."

"You'll make new friends," I told him while glancing over my shoulder.

"Find other guys to watch football with."

"Maybe," he muttered, tucking the ball under his arm and wrenching open the fridge door, "but they'll all be Patriot's fans. Fucking cheats."

"Devon."

"Sorry," he muttered an apology over the curse I didn't allow in the house and pulled out the milk. "The name's Dillon, remember?"

"Not at home, it's not." I frowned as he pulled a box of cereal from the cabinet. "You just ate breakfast."

"Yeah, but I'm starved again."

I shook my head and turned on the hot water. Teenage boys, I'd found, would eat a single mom out of house and home.

Home.

I swallowed against the sudden tightening in my throat. We no longer had a home. The rental we'd been tossed into didn't have that sense of peace or comfort one should. More than anything, I wanted that for Devon to make our transition as easy as possible even though he seemed unfazed by the move except for having to relocate in Patriot's Nation. Not that we'd had a say in the matter.

The pre-season had kicked off two days earlier, and even though his adored Jet's hadn't been playing and his best friends weren't with us, I'd gone all out with the wings, nachos, and chili. While he'd been vocal in his appreciation for what I'd done, he hadn't been able to keep the sadness off his face.

Devon crunched on cereal at the table behind me as the mower continued outside and I washed dishes.

I allowed myself a moment to fantasize, placing myself and that hot neighbor in a fairy tale romance like the book I'd lost myself in the night before. Reading had become my escape, my neighbor became the man I imagined behind the author's words.

The hero.

The knight in shining armor.

The man who would love my son as much as I did.

Letting out a heavy sigh, I rinsed the last plate and unplugged the sink to drain the dirty, sudsy water. Temptation to glance out the window rose, but I squashed it down, burying my need for physical touch. Affection. Someone telling me I had worth beyond being a mom.

At least I had *that*, though. Devon was my life.

I shut the kitchen window against the rising heat outside without looking at him, and forcing a smile, I dried my hands and turned to find my son pouring more milk over another pile of cereal. "I just bought that box yesterday."

"Should have gotten two of 'em," he said around a mouthful.

I crossed my arms and leaned against the counter, my smile coming easier. My son, the love of my life, looked nothing like the loser sperm-donor I'd hooked up with at a bar sixteen years earlier. He'd been red-headed with light eyes, just how I liked my men. Gingers were my weakness, but as time wore on, I'd been pleased Devon looked like me with his blond hair and dark eyes.

I did feel bad that Devon didn't have a father figure growing up, so when I'd met my ex ten years earlier, I thought maybe he would be the one. The perfect man for me, the perfect father for Devon. Turned out that thinking was far from right.

So damn far we had to uproot and start our lives over.

"What are your plans for today?" I asked, ready to change my train of thought off the depression that clung to the back of my mind with cat-like claws, sharp and digging.

"Dunno." Devon slurped down the milk from his bowl. "Probably head outside before it gets too hot."

While he'd been outside quite a bit, checking out the neighborhood on his bike, I'd been staying inside mostly. After what we'd been through, I would have preferred keeping him on lock down, too, but I couldn't do that to a teenage boy who loved to socialize, smile, and keep active.

I'd been like that once upon a time, too.

"You've been doing that every day," I said with yet another feigned smile as my heart ached in my chest. "Sure there isn't something else of interest drawing you out? Girl next door kinda thing?"

"Pfft. Nah." He stood, his lanky limbs unfolding, putting him at eye level with me.

While I stood at five-foot-seven and fuller all over than I'd have preferred, he was a bone rack, still in the middle of puberty that I hoped would eventually fill him in and give him more height like his biological father.

He'd been a big man—again, how I liked them.

"Boy next door?" I asked without a hint of judgement in my voice. God knew there wasn't anything we hadn't talked about before.

"No, *Mom*. I told you I'm not into boys."

"It wouldn't matter to me if you were," I said with a smile, never being more serious in my life.

His dark eyes shone with the grin lifting his lips. "I know. Got stuff to make your chocolate chip cookies?"

Of course he'd go right back to food.

"Yep." I grabbed his cereal bowl and spoon off the table while he put away the milk.

"You ought to take some to that guy mowing his lawn out back."

I jerked my head toward Devon, one eyebrow raised.

Devon shrugged, his crooked smirk so damn adorable my heart melted. "Reverse welcome to the neighborhood kinda thing," he explained, his dimple popping again as his eyes twinkled. *"He's a ginger."*

I flicked water from the sink at him like one would to an annoying cat, and he flinched, laughing. "Hey! Nothing wrong with being neighborly."

Yeah, my mind had already gone way beyond that route even though I knew that's not what Devon referred to. Getting close, though, meant letting down walls and being forced with the decision on whether or not I could trust a man again.

For the sake of my son, I refused to do so. My heart would stay safer that way, too.

"You make them, I'll drop them off," Devon said when I didn't answer. "He's got a Harley."

I carefully placed his clean bowl in the dish rack to my right. Devon had always been into motorcycles. My ex had bought him one the year before, promising to fix the old bike up with him. Empty promises had led to Devon learning to tinker on engines on his own. He'd gotten the old thing running, but that, too, had been left behind.

Swallowing the thickness in my throat I'd become too damn familiar with the previous couple of months, I didn't bother with a smile while turning to grip my son's bony shoulders.

Eyes, dark as mine peered at me, and it killed me I had to break his heart yet again.

"You need to stay away from men like him," I whispered, unable to force more strength to my vocal cords. "We ended up in this mess because I didn't."

"Wasn't your fault, Mom," Devon said. "He was a fucking asshole, and until you knew that, we were in too deep."

Tears welled in my eyes, hazing my vision of my beautiful boy. I cupped his cheek, hating the hint of scruff beneath my palm. Choosing to ignore the curse I didn't appreciate in my house, I forced that damn smile—for him.

"Learn from my mistakes, Dev. Make better choices than I did."

"You didn't know," he insisted.

"But I should have gotten you out of there at the first sign."

His smirk tilted and he gave me a quick, uncomfortable hug.

"Ew." I wrinkled my nose even while soaking in the tiniest bit of affection he offered. While we shared secrets without embarrassment, he wasn't as huggy as he'd been as a younger boy. "You need a shower before heading out to see that neighborhood girl."

"Mom," he groaned out, turning away, but I caught the pink in his cheeks.

"And wear the shorts that don't sag halfway down your ass!" I hollered at his retreating form while the football once more found itself tossed into the air. "Oh, and shut the windows and turn on the AC unit in the living room, will ya? It's getting hot outside!"

"Yeah!"

Heaviness weighed on my shoulders as Devon disappeared around the corner. Letting him go, allowing him to make his own choices, good or bad, killed me. The not knowing of what danger lurked, of who might recognize us and tell the wrong person, kept me awake more often than not.

A clunk, and the old AC window unit ground to life from the living room. Like the rest of the ranch house, it was a piece of shit but managed to keep the day time hours cooler than the sweltering August air outside. Day four of an unforeseeable ending fore-casted heat wave—and I prayed like hell the damn thing wouldn't shit the bed.

Dark circles still clung beneath my eyes, I noted an hour later while peering in our lone bathroom's medicine cabinet mirror. Shitty lighting didn't help matters, but I couldn't blame that for my sallow-looking complexion, either. Dark, tired eyes. Brows in desperate need of a wax job. Two stress pimples on my forehead—at least I had long, sweeping bangs to hide the damn things, even if they were a mousy, dark brown rather than the golden locks I preferred.

Dev wasn't the only one who needed a shower and shave. I'd gone a few days without a proper pampering, and even though I didn't have a reason for doing so, I decided some self-care wouldn't go to waste.

At least I would feel better about myself.

I plugged up the stained tub and creaked on the faucet to fill it to the brim. Not nearly as deep, nor did it have the jets of the one I'd left back at home—

"That's no longer home," I whispered, needing to remind myself yet again. "This is the new reality, *Michelle*. Best deal with it."

Sliding into the hot water soothed my body, but not my mind.

At least I had the neighbor to fantasize over.

Come the following Monday, though, I would begin my new job as a janitor at the retirement home two blocks away. I had the marshal to thank for the thirty hours a week job that came with benefits. A much needed way to support us since I hadn't been able to empty my ex's safe like I'd planned to do before shit went down.

We had left the west coast with what we wore and one backpack each. Lingering would have put our lives in even greater danger.

"I'm heading out!" Devon hollered from somewhere in the house.

"Don't go too far and keep your cell on you!"

His muttered, "Yeah, yeah," reached my ears seconds before the door slammed shut behind him.

Overwhelming need to get out of the tub and keep an eye on my son coursed through me, but the marshal overseeing us had told me no one had been hurt while under their protection.

There could always be a first.

I pushed the thought aside and went back to Mr. Ginger, the mighty fine beast of a neighbor I couldn't keep from stirring my body to life.

3

VIGIL

The fucking heat sucked donkey dick. I should have gotten my ass out of bed to finish the mowing a few hours earlier before the sun got too high. Damn ball of fire beat down on my head when I moved to the front yard, my chest and back already dripping sweat even though I'd taken a few water breaks while finishing up the backyard.

Nothing worse than mowing. I'd gotten that chore shoved at me when Ricky and I had moved in with Auntie Jeanie, and I'd been doing it non-fucking stop ever since. I'd had about enough.

I caught sight of someone in my periphery and turned to see who it was. The new punk neighbor with the hot mom. I cut the engine while telling myself I wasn't interested.

"Hey!" I called out as he peddled closer.

His brow furrowed and shoulders tensed, but he braked, putting one foot onto the road in front of my house and nodded. Dark, wary eyes studied me, something I could appreciate in a soon-to-be man.

I swiped my forearm across my sweaty forehead. "Interested in making a few bucks every week?"

The wariness intensified, and he glanced beyond me at my house. "Well, sir, it depends on what it is."

Respectful—guess he wasn't a punk after all. "Mowing my fucking yard. I'm too old for this shit."

He turned his focus back on my face. "Front and back?"

I had a huge fucking backyard. "Yeah. Once a week or more if it needs it. I'll pay you fifty bucks, you use my mower, and I provide the gas. What do you say? Help an old bastard out?"

He did a quick once-over me before turning his attention on the one garage door I'd left gaping open. "You got a Harley," he said, nodding his chin toward my bike.

"Yeah," I answered even though he hadn't asked a question.

"You just ride it or tinker, too?"

A slow grin stretched my lips. The boy might be

straight-faced, but he couldn't hide the interest in his eyes. "I know a thing or two about engines."

He tore his focus off my bike and turned it back on me, his shoulders slumped as he let out a heavy breath. "I'll mow your lawn, sir."

I strode forward and offered my hand, clinching our deal the old fashioned way. "Name's Frankie, but everyone calls me Vigil."

He clasped my hand with a decent grip, holding my gaze like a man. "De—Dillon."

A slip up—a fucking lie, his flitting away gaze told me. "Nice to meet you, Dillon. New to the neighborhood, right?" I asked, releasing his hand.

"Yeah. Mom and I moved in behind you a couple weeks ago."

Just the two of them—not that I truly cared even though I'd busted a nut the night before over thoughts of his mom's ass.

"That ranch is Widow Betsy's place. Or used to be. She passed a couple months ago." I frowned, memories of her sweet smile and watery green eyes always lighting whenever I checked in on her coming to mind.

"Yeah?" Dillion, or whatever his real name was, asked.

"She was like a grandma to me. Took care of her

and her lawn." Not that I missed that part at all. "I pretty much look after everyone in our neighborhood, though."

"Why's that?" He peered at me as though trying to figure me out while gripping his handlebars tight.

"Natural instinct to look after those around me—friends, family, neighbors." I shrugged and swiped at the droplet of sweat running down into my beard. "That makes you part of my tribe, Dillon."

His lips quirked at the corner, that interest sparking in his eyes again. "Cool."

"Welcome to the neighborhood."

"Thanks."

"Where you from?"

Dillon shifted his focus onto the mower, completely shutting down. "Out west."

Vague, but not a lie from what I could tell. "You like motorcycles, I take it."

"Yeah."

"Come on." I turned toward my garage without looking to see if he followed, noting the dirt on my black truck in the driveway on my way there. The thing needed to be washed... I'd do that next and spray myself down to cool the fuck off. Maybe I'd put a pool out back next spring—my yard was big enough for one. Less lawn to mow...

I damn near wilted in relief when I stepped into the coolness of the garage. Fucking shade had never felt so good.

"That's my everyday bike," I told Dillon when he sauntered in behind me, pointing at my chromed-out and shiny Fat Boy. "And this," I pulled a tarp off the old bike I had on my lift, "is my baby."

"Holy shit! Is that a Peashooter?" Dillon crowded close, checking the bike out, his grin catching enough my lips twitched in response.

I stepped out of his way and crossed my arms. "It's a '28. Found it on my friend's property up in Maine."

He leaned close, checking out the frame I'd been cleaning up. "This is so cool!"

I nodded, enjoying the kid's enthusiasm as he inspected the bike like he wanted to make me an offer on the damn thing.

"I had an old Shovelhead back home," he said quietly as though to himself while straightening and pressed his lips tight like he'd said too much.

"Yeah?"

Dillon hesitated a second before nodding. "Do you box?" he asked, nodding toward the other side of my garage outfitted with weights, a heavy bag, and speed bag.

"Just to keep my old ass in shape. I use the weights more than the bags these days. Getting too old for that shit, too."

Dillon eyed me once more with that wariness as though trying to get a read on me. I didn't have jack shit to hide like he obviously did so I didn't bother to shut my face down cold like I usually did if people got too damn nosey.

"You're welcome to come over and work out whenever you want," I offered.

"You mean that?"

"Yeah, sure." I shrugged. "Since you're new in town, I can't imagine you've got too many friends yet. Going to the local high school in a couple weeks?"

Dillon nodded while moving to the heavy bag and threw a punch that definitely needed work. "Could you show me how to fight?"

I narrowed my gaze, catching that wary vibe radiate off him again as he refused to make eye contact. "Think it's going to be a rough transition into the new school?"

"Doesn't hurt to be prepared," he said, his voice low.

"Play any sports?"

"I played freshman football last year, but it's too

late for me to try out for the new school's team for this season."

"I played back in high school. Lineman. You?"

"Running back."

The kid had skinny-ass legs for a running back. He must have mad speed and moves. "You want to play ball here, you're gonna have to put on some muscle—even if you run like a goddamn gazelle."

He nodded absently while glancing around my garage again, his gaze lingering on my cut I had tossed over the work bench's vise. His shoulders hunched as though the weight of the world rested on them. With just him and his mom, I expected he felt like the man of the house. Add moving across the country, and I expected the poor kid was hurting. I found myself rubbing my chest.

"Tell you what," I said, "on top of the mowing, you help me out rebuilding the Peashooter, and I'll give you a key to the side door there so you can come and go as you please. Tinkering or lifting."

Dillion's head jerked toward me, excitement returning to his dark eyes. "You would do that? You don't even know me."

"I'm good at reading people, Dillon. You seem like a good kid. Respectful."

He let out a small laugh. "That's cuz of my mom. I sass off, and she usually cuffs me upside the head."

I grinned, remembering Auntie Jeanie doing the same to both Ricky and me. "Your mom sounds like a good woman."

"The best," he didn't hesitate to say before turning to face me fully and letting out a heavy exhale as though coming to a serious conclusion in his brain. "You like watching football?"

"I tend to sit my ass in front of the TV all day Sunday during the season, yeah."

"Patriots fan?"

"Of course."

Dillion rolled his eyes and groaned. "Figures. I'm a Jet's fan."

I barked a laugh. "We still cool?" I asked, sticking out my hand.

It took him a few seconds, but he offered a sheepish grin and clasped my hand. "Yeah."

"You're welcome to come over Sunday to watch the day's games with me if you want. I got a wicked cool man cave in the basement."

"Wicked?"

"It's a Boston thing. Adjective for everything from weather to fried clams."

"Oh" Dillion glanced over at my cut again.

"Mom probably wouldn't want me over here without meeting you first. Mowing *or* lifting weights and boxing. How about you come to our place on Sunday? She makes a mean chili and nachos."

Good food, a single woman with what seemed like a great kid... *I'm not interested*, I reminded myself I'd never wanted kids, blood or adopted. "Sure, I'd love to. What can I bring?"

"Mom would say nothing, so I'll go with that."

"I'll be there—if it's okay with her."

He grinned, a dimple showing in his cheek. "I know how to get my way."

I chuckled, and Dillion shoved his hands in his jean short's pockets, his bony shoulders hunching again. "I gotta get going—Mom's probably wondering where the hell I am."

"Sure thing."

I watched Dillion hurry back to his bike, my mind rolling at a steady clip. Good looking kid—I wondered if he got his looks from his mom. I also wondered over his lies and what made him feel the need for them.

While I usually hated liars, something about the kid tugged at my heart.

Absently rubbing my chest, I watched his skinny

ass climb aboard his bike like it was a chopper, and he its master.

He waved and took off into the heat.

I went back out into the sun to finish the two rows I had left, cursing non-fucking stop at the damn sun. In a few months I'd be cursing the snow, but there was no way in hell I'd ever leave my life for somewhere with less volatile weather.

My club, my blood brother, even if he ended up getting the boot, and my Viper brothers—they were everything to me. I wouldn't let anything happen to any of them, and I sure as fuck wasn't going to leave them of my own volition.

4
———

MILA

I chewed off my thumb nail while watching the front windows, head swiveling side to side waiting for Devon to ride into view. The neighborhood was quiet with a dozen or so houses, so I had no clue what he did all those hours while riding around.

He should have been back by now.

My stomach twisted tight. I did *not* want to be a helicopter parent. I wanted Devon to have his freedom, but my inner protective nature over my only child fought tooth and nail. I'd been doing my best to give him space, but it was hard. I know I failed more often than not.

A rush of breath left me as he came around the corner, peddling lazily through the sticky afternoon.

I yanked open the door the second his foot hit the stoop, the August air blasting my face like a damn furnace. "Where have you been? It's been three hours!"

Flushed, he'd been smiling until my outburst. His lips flatlined as he walked up the steps. "Just riding, Mom. Met a few neighbors, not like I'm out joining a gang or running drugs."

I stepped back, letting him into the cooler interior of the house and locked up tight behind him. "You have to be careful! I tried texting you a few times. I told you to keep your cell on you."

"Yeah." He pulled it from the back of his jean shorts pocket. "Had the ringer off. Sorry. Hey, did you make those cookies?" he asked, shoving the cell back into his pocket and flashing his dimple at me while wiping perspiration off his forehead.

He knew what that dimple did to me, the little turd. I let out a sigh and waved for him to follow me into the kitchen. "Yeah."

His butt wasn't even in the chair before he dug into the plateful I'd set out for him two hours earlier. I grabbed a glass and the milk before he could ask.

"Is this all you made?" he asked, glancing behind him at the kitchen counter. "I was gonna take some over to Vigil."

"Who's Vigil?"

"Neighbor guy I met earlier." Devon washed down a mouthful of cookie with his milk. "He hired me to mow his lawn. Fifty bucks once a week!"

"Yeah?" I leaned against the counter, my own emotions easily swayed by the excitement in his voice.

"Yeah—he's got like a full gym in his garage, heavy bags and all. He's gonna help me put on some weight for next football season. Teach me how to fight, too."

Devon had never been anything but a lover, but I understood his desire to learn how to wield his fists.

"Okay," I agreed even though he hadn't exactly asked permission. "So who is this guy?"

"Your ginger."

My heart stalled out but kicked back in at a heightened speed. "The biker?"

Devon eyed me while shoving another entire cookie into his mouth. "He was real honest, no filter, Mom. I got a good vibe from him, and I felt like shit lying to him about my name."

"Well he's a biker, so he's a liar, too," I stated with finality.

"He rides with the Vipers."

No. Way. I stilled, every muscle in my body

instantly strung tight as hell. "How did you find that out?" I asked, my tone as wary as my mind.

"Saw his cut in the garage."

Silence hovered between us as he finished off his cookies and milk and I forced myself to relax. Breathe. "We left that all behind us, Dev," I finally said. "Fresh start."

"Fresh start," Devon agreed with a nod. "That means you take him a plate of cookies and see for yourself that he's different."

"Absolutely not."

"Fine, then I'll take him the damn cookies."

"Devon."

"Sorry." He offered a sheepish grin with that dimple, but I didn't allow cursing in the house. "How about I take him the cookies and he can bring back the plate on Sunday and stay to watch football with us?"

My eyebrow shot up. "How long were you over there at his house, Devon Zeigler?"

"The name's Dillon Evans," he said with a grin while standing and meeting me eye to eye. "And Vigil is a good man."

I narrowed my gaze, arms crossing tight over my chest while I studied my son. God knew he'd seen enough shit in his fifteen years to have the intuition of an adult, but I wasn't having it. "No."

"Come on, Mom," he whined, rolling his eyes. "You gotta give him a chance. He's a biker, yeah, but he's a good man. You don't trust anyone but me—so *trust* me, okay? He's not some asshole who's going to take advantage of you. I could tell that within five minutes of talking to him."

"I *do* trust you."

"Then let this play out. Please, Mom." He swallowed, and the pain in his eyes tore my insides to shreds. "Vigil is the first friend I've made here."

"He's too old to be your friend."

"That's bullshit and you know it."

"Dev—"

"Come *on*, Mom. I know this is asking a lot considering the bullshit behind us, but let it ride out."

Our stare down lasted too long, and I caved to his pain rather than the dimple he didn't pull out of his bag of tricks again. "Fine. Take him the cookies and invite him to watch the games with us, but I'll reserve my own judgement for after I meet him."

"Anyone ever tell you you're wicked cool?"

"Wicked, huh?" I laughed lightly even though I was far from happy.

"It's a Boston thing."

"Yeah. I know."

He grinned and grabbed the plastic-covered plate behind me, landing a quick smack of lips on my cheek. "Thanks!"

"Hey!" I called after him as he scooted for the back door. "That's all I made!"

"You can make me some more tomorrow!"

I huffed a snort as the back door slammed shut behind him, but couldn't stay put. Telling myself I needed to keep an eye on him, I followed him outside and remained on the back porch while he loped across the yard toward Mr. Ginger's—Vigil, the *biker*.

A shiver licked down my spine despite the stifling heat, but I couldn't decide if the feeling was pleasant or not. I went with the latter considering all I'd lived through the previous ten years.

Devon knocked on Vigil's back slider rather than go around front, and Vigil slid it open within seconds leading me to believe he'd been right inside.

He towered over Devon by at least half a foot if not more. With shoulders twice as wide and easily three times as thick as my son's, the man was a beast. He'd put on a black t-shirt and wore cut-off sweats.

Nothing like a man in sweats.

My mouth flooded with drool as I wished for a closer view—but I wrapped my arms around myself the second he glanced beyond Devon toward our house. At that distance, I couldn't make out what they said or much more than the fact Vigil's eyes were light, but definite energy rippled across our backyards, tightening my nipples.

Damn it all to hell and then some.

I turned and let myself back in the house, hoping Devon would hurry so I could lock up behind him.

5

VIGIL

Rather than wariness, a sheepish grin plastered on Dillon's face as he handed me a plate of cookies. "From my mom. She makes the best chocolate chip cookies ever."

"Thanks." I took the plate and glanced across the yards and bushes separating ours.

A dark haired woman stood on their back stoop watching us like a hawk. Protective momma bear—and my dick twitched even though I couldn't make her out all that well. She hugged herself and turned away, slipping into the house without a wave, same as Monday night.

"We still on for Sunday?" I asked, returning my focus on Dillon and grabbing a cookie from beneath the wrap to shove in my mouth.

"Yep."

"Damn, that's good," I said around my mouthful.

He grinned, his eyes lighting up like a little kid. "Told ya."

"Sure it's okay with your mom? I don't want to impose." I didn't add in the obvious closed-off vibe I'd gotten from her seconds earlier.

"It's cool. She said I can mow for you, but wants to meet you before I can hang out and shit."

I nodded, chewing the second cookie I stuffed into my mouth. "I'd invite her over now, but I'm about to head to my club for the night."

"MC?"

Studying his face didn't reveal jack shit as he held my stare. "Vicious Vipers. Heard of them?"

He finally glanced away. "No, sir."

Liar. "You tell your mom—what's her name?"

"Michelle."

"You tell her I'll be over Sunday."

"Yes, sir." Dillon turned and walked off.

"Lawn is gonna need mowing Friday or Saturday," I called after him, not wanting to do that shit even though the forecast said it'd be cooler by the weekend.

He turned and walked backward, giving me a mock salute. "I'll talk her into it."

Or, I could just take the plate I'd have emptied before morning back over the next day. Meet the wary mom, find out who'd actually moved into my neighborhood, and hopefully put her mind at ease.

In the meantime, I planned to call Devil and see what he could dig up on the single mom and her lying son.

———

I got news Ricky sobered up on Tuesday, but he skipped our weekly meeting on Wednesday. Add in the fact my tech nerd brother couldn't find anything beyond a cable and electric bill under the name Michelle Evans, and aggravation ate at my stomach.

Nothing, Devil had claimed. Not a damn thing, like she and her son Dillon didn't exist at all. That told me one thing for certain. Michelle Evans wasn't her real name, same as I'd suspected of the name her son had given me. The second thing I expected, she was on the run or had been placed in my neighborhood on purpose.

But whose purpose?

The FBI in order to get close to me and the Vipers, or for her own safety? The wariness from both

Michelle and Dillon led me to believe the latter rather than an undercover operation. Being in my neighborhood put them under my protection, exactly as I'd told Dillon, so I wasn't going to rest until I learned the truth.

I waited until he mowed my front yard Friday morning before taking the plate back to his mom so I could get her alone. At least she'd agreed to let him mow without meeting me first.

She cracked open the back door, face pale and dark eyes full of emotion—namely fear, solidifying my thoughts on her situation. She definitely wasn't with the FBI. No one could fake that kind of wariness.

My smile came easier, but also because she was so damn beautiful with lush dark hair and eyes the color of golden chestnuts. "Morning."

She glanced beyond me, definitely hearing my mower still running out front before opening the door a little wider. Turning her focus back on me, she eyed me like a skittish cat.

I didn't want to be a gentleman, but forced myself to keep my focus on her face rather than check her out.

"Thanks for the cookies." I handed her the plate, giving her a reason to let her white-knuckled grip on the door release. "Best I've had since my Auntie Jeanie's."

Her lips quirked, and she rubbed her palms down her shorts before taking the plate without touching my fingers. "Glad you liked them. I'm Michelle. Dillon's mom." Her husky voice kicked me in the groin with a shot of pure, fucking lust.

She didn't offer her hand, so I didn't either. "Vigil."

"Thanks for giving him a job."

I shrugged, studying her face with the color returning to pinken her cheeks. The wariness in her eyes remained even as her gaze flitted down over my chest really quick. "He's a good kid. Hope you don't mind I invited him to make himself at home with my weights and shit in the garage. Figured he could use a friend."

Michelle studied me, her dark eyes intent, her full lips pressed into a flat line. I didn't move under her scrutiny, letting her see whatever she wished. I wasn't ashamed of what—who—I was. If she had something against bikers or big fuckers like me, that was her problem, not mine.

"He *is* a good kid," she finally said, her voice still low and sexy as fuck, "but I don't want him getting caught up in the wrong crowd."

My turn to study her even though I knew exactly what her words meant. She definitely had a thing against bikers, no doubt. "I might be a biker," I said, "but we don't deal drugs. I don't even allow my brothers to do drugs beyond smoking a bit of pot."

"Your brothers."

Not a question, but I felt the need to answer, let her know exactly who lived behind her. "I'm the president of the Viper's Boston chapter."

Her face paled again, and she swallowed. "You're the leader of a biker gang."

"I am."

"You're *exactly* the type of crowd I don't want my son getting caught up in," she snipped, her eyes taking on a glint that swelled my dick. Fuck, did I like my women snippy and wild.

"I'm also exactly the type of man who can help the kid out," I argued, bringing a flush to her cheeks that stiffened me to the point of discomfort. "He wants to get stronger. Learn how to protect himself. He also needs someone he can turn to if shit goes bad like he seems to think it might at the new school." I considered the dipshit punks I knew who supposedly ran the high school's pecking order and thought that Dillon might have to put up with that exact shit until he found his place.

Michelle glared up at me, and god*damn* did I like the pissed look on her face. Tense silence grew between us, but I let her have the time to war out whatever went on inside her head. Her lush, dark hair hung around her shoulders in gentle waves, falling over more than a handful of tits. The t-shirt covering her upper body hid whatever figure lay beneath those tits, but the thighs below her shorts and curvy calves told me all I needed to.

Michelle Evans was all woman, the kind a man with my size could enjoy without restraint. The memory of her round ass had me biting back a groan, and I dragged my focus back to her face without realizing I'd been checking her out.

"Are you done?" she asked, that snippy tone sending a rush through me. *Nothing* better than a wildcat.

"Unless you're offering to turn around and let me check out the backside, too." Fire lit her eyes into obsidian as her lips pursed, and I chuckled. "You're hot as fuck, Michelle. Can't blame a man for noticing."

"You won't talk about your club with my son," she tossed out, choosing to ignore my compliments.

I nodded, thankful she hadn't told me to fuck off and leave them alone. "If that's what you want."

"You won't invite him to ride with you."

"I won't."

Her chin tilted upward as she tried to peer down her nose at me even though I stood close to a foot taller than her. "No booze or drugs."

"Definitely not."

"And keep the cursing to a minimum."

I snorted. "Can't promise you anything on that one, wildcat."

She glared, and my dick enjoyed every goddamn second of the tension between us. "*No hitting on me.*"

One of my eyebrows raised on its own. "Not even a little?"

"The last thing I want is to get involved with any man, let alone an outlaw biker."

"Who said anything about being an outlaw?" I shot back, crossing my arms, enjoying myself way too much.

She glanced down at my straining pecs and jerked her focus back upward—she couldn't hide the hint of interest in her eyes, though. "You're a Viper which means you're a one-percenter."

Michelle Evans knew what the average American didn't. She'd just dropped a hint into her past Devil hadn't been able to uncover.

"Being a one-percenter doesn't mean we hurt

innocent people in any way," I said, my own voice lowering.

"It still means criminal activity."

"There's a fine line between black and white," I argued once more, keeping my tone level even though her judging me set me off in some way that I usually didn't give a shit about. I wanted her to like me. Trust me. I told myself it was for her son's sake and not my desire to strip her down to see what lay beneath her unflattering clothes.

"There *is* a gray area," she agreed, glancing behind me as my mower shut off. She let out a heavy exhale. "My son and his safety is all I'm interested in right now, Vigil." Returning her focus to my face, she let me see some of her vulnerability in her dark eyes.

"Understood."

Tight lipped, she nodded.

"So, will you allow me to be his friend?" I asked, needing her permission since I expected Dillon wouldn't listen anyway if she told him to stay away from me. The kid was definitely drawn to me enough to test her—and I actually liked the kid.

"You've offered him too much to keep him away."

My turn to nod, letting her know we were on the same page thought-wise. I unfolded my arms, dropping them to my sides. "Wasn't my intent when I first met him, but his interest in bikes and wanting to learn how to defend himself wasn't something I could ignore since I got bullied as a kid. I can offer him that, Michelle, and even without getting him involved in my club, I've got the connections to help you keep him out of trouble."

But why the hell I wanted to, I had no fucking clue. I found myself rubbing my chest. Did I have a rash growing beneath my skin or something? Grimacing, I dropped my hand.

Another prolonged silence rose between us while she warred, holding my stare with more balls than most men.

"Are you coming over on Sunday to watch football with him?" she finally asked.

"If the invitation is still good."

"At the first sign of trouble, you're out of his life, neighbor or not."

"Deal." I stuck out my hand.

She eyed it for a few seconds before sliding her palm against mine.

Instant lust shot to my dick, jerking my length in my jeans. Her grip was soft and warm. Feminine yet firm. I wondered what those fingers would feel like wrapped around my dick.

"See you Sunday," I said, releasing her hand and

turning before she caught an eyeful of my hard-on. Sure, I wanted to bury my dick in her ass, but I found myself wanting to prove myself to her even more. I wanted her to look at me like Dillon did—with fucking awe and appreciation. I wanted her to trust me to not lead her son astray, for her to know I had his best interests in mind when offering to help the kid out.

Why?

I had no fucking clue, but I was going to roll with it. If nothing else, I could feel good about myself for looking after yet another family in my neighborhood.

On a hunch, I texted Devil after Dillon took off for the day, letting him know Michelle Evans might have a connection to a one-percenter club.

He gave me a thumbs up emoji and nothing else. The waiting fucking sucked.

6

MILA

Vigil had won my son over, heart and soul. He didn't stop talking about him all week long. From Peashooter to speed bags and back again, Devon kept up a running infomercial for the man. He'd also called him my ginger twice more before I put a stop to it.

Jaded through and through, I wouldn't ever allow a man in my heart ever again. Couldn't do so without trusting, something I *knew* I would never do.

The biker next door might have won my son over, but he wouldn't scale my walls—knight or no knight. I hated the fact that his true colors, pun definitely intended, would eventually shine through and Devon would end up crushed, but I couldn't bring myself to prohibit him from seeing the first friend he'd made.

School would begin in a matter of weeks, and he'd find new friends. I hoped Vigil would eventually take a back seat to those closer to Devon's own age, ones going through the same stages in life, falling for the same teenage girls.

A shudder rippled through me as I brushed my teeth while readying for bed Saturday night.

Girls.

I was thankful as hell he hadn't been interested in them before we'd left home. The heartbreak of leaving a first love behind wouldn't have crushed just him. I still would have made the same choices, though. I would have stood up for truth in exchange for leniency and safety for my son.

The smaller window unit in the tiny master bedroom grumbled as much as the one in the living room, but at least it kept the temperature decent enough to sleep. The humidity had passed, but it was still too hot to sleep with the windows open. Not that I would, anyway. Fear kept them locked tight, same as the doors whenever we were inside.

Hoping nightmares and worry wouldn't plague me like usual, I crawled between the scratchy sheets, once more missing the satin I'd left behind.

Fresh start, I told myself while closing my eyes. Complaining or lamenting what I'd given up wouldn't gain me a damn thing.

Vigil came to mind, same as he always did whenever I laid down and closed my eyes. Who was I kidding? He entered my brain a lot while they were open, too. The damn man in all his blue-gray eyed hotness annoyed the hell out of me by turning my body on the way he did.

I liked them big. He certainly fit that bill.

I liked them strong with a no-nonsense, no-bull-shit attitude. I didn't question that about Vigil either even though we'd only spoken that one time.

I also liked them empathetic and protective. Vigil seemed to be both and much more, but I didn't trust him to remain so.

I'd known men like him before, and allowing myself to be vulnerable had only ended in heartache and pain.

Vigil would be inside our walls the next day for the time of two football games. Nervousness ate at my stomach, and I tossed beneath the sheet, turning onto my back to stare at the dark ceiling.

The image of him stayed fresh in my mind, though, warming my entire body from hair to toes, damn him.

Frowning, I cursed his name a few times in my head while need dampened between my thighs and tightened my nipples. I refused to give into my baser instincts. I refused to touch myself while haunted by a man whose nature shouldn't turn me on. I refused myself release even if he was hot as hell and checked off every damn box in my make-me-wet list.

Nope.

I flopped over, punched my pillow, and clamped my eyes shut.

Tomorrow, I will ignore his body, his eyes, and the color of his hair. I will focus on Dev and making my son happy.

That's all that truly mattered.

———

"Just because I'm allowing him over here doesn't mean I fully approve," I told Devon the next morning while he emptied yet another box of cereal into his bowl. "We left that behind us for a new start, and having Vigil as your friend isn't new, Dev."

"He's not an asshole," Devon reminded me of what he'd first said about the man, frowning from across the table.

"Maybe not, but I can't do this again."

Devon rolled his eyes. "I'm not suggesting you sleep with the guy, Mom."

"Devon!"

"What?" He shrugged. "He's your type, but I want him as a friend. I need him, Mom. He's going to let me use his gym. Teach me how to box so I can protect you if that asshole ever makes parole and comes after us."

Tears hazed my vision and clogged my throat. My little man wanting to be a big man too soon. Could I love him any more than I already did? Saying no seemed damn near impossible, even without his flashing his dimple at me. "At the first red flag, he's out of your life. Understand? I made a horrible mistake once and I won't do it again."

"He's a good man. I know it. Give him a chance to prove it."

I didn't respond. Devon knew how I felt about trusting anyone but him.

"You know he cared for the widow who lived here before us?" Devon continued with the infomercial he always took up whenever the subject of Vigil came up. "He cares for everyone in the neighborhood. Calls us all his tribe."

His tribe. So his protective nature went beyond his Viper brotherhood. I chewed on that fact while

Devon finished his cereal and I drank down the last of my coffee, ignoring the crust of my cold, buttered toast sitting on the napkin in front of me.

I hated that I looked forward to his coming over. I hated who he was on the outside.

Would his inside self be enough to sway me into allowing Devon his friendship? A huge part of me hoped for it. Another huge part of me wanted him to look at me like he had in the doorway earlier in the week.

Hunger.

Lust.

The kind that created the massive bulge I'd caught a peek of—but he'd turned away without pursuing or trying to draw attention to that fact. What asshole biker did that?

None I'd known. Even my ex's brothers hadn't treated others' old ladies with respect. He'd shared me a few times too many, not that I'd had a say in the matter.

But I do now, and I won't be used again. I won't be hurt again, and neither will Dev.

Standing, I shoved thoughts of my ex to the back of my mind. He was part of our past—and perhaps Vigil would be a part in our future. But as my son's friend only. I'd had my share of alpha assholes and their cocks they thought women existed to suck.

Someday I might even move on enough to touch myself to thoughts of a decent man, but that wouldn't be any time soon.

Vigil's arrival at the front door a few hours later definitely pushed me in the self-release direction. He wore another tight, black t-shirt that encased his hot upper body, revealing dips and valleys of muscle with every move he made. The man knew how to wear a pair of jeans, too, tight in all the right places.

Good God almighty.

Big everywhere, just like that glimpse the day before had awarded me. My heart raced and palms sweated.

"Dillon said not to bring anything, but my Auntie Jeanie taught me better," he said, handing over a bag of chips and store-bought brownies, jerking my focus from where it had wandered. Better than the six-pack of beer I'd expected him to show up with.

"Th-thank you. Come on in."

Caught staring ... damn him.

I'd gone with my usual nondescript clothing, not wanting to snag his attention, but he still gave me that once-over while stepping past me into the living room. Tingles raced over my skin, and I fought off goosebumps and the hard nipples I wouldn't be able to explain away from being chilly, since the damn AC could barely keep the returned heat outside at bay.

Devon came hurrying down the hallway. "Hey, Vigil!"

The two shared a bro hug, back slaps and all, and when my son pulled away, a grin of excitement and something else filled his face, something I hadn't seen for months ... hope.

My heart squeezed in my chest. Vigil brought hope into our house, and I fought its effects on my own body and mind while taking the snacks he'd brought into the kitchen. What felt like life stirred inside me for the first time in what seemed forever, every inch of me aware of the raw masculinity of him. Even from the kitchen, his voice rippled over me like a zapping live wire, setting me on edge.

With a long inhale and exhale, I fought for calm and forced myself to return to the living room and settled into the lone chair Vigil's widow friend must have spent hours in. The damn seat sank in the middle, but it molded to my backside perfectly, worn-in and comfortable.

Vigil and Devon sat on the couch facing the TV,

both laughing and bullshitting, spouting off stats and the stuff I never paid attention to. All I knew was football players wore tight pants and a lot of them ended up with concussions while trying to get goals —or whatever they called them.

I found myself smiling, unable to tear my gaze off my son as the first game started. To see him so free, so relaxed and happy... Tears hazed my vision of him, and I excused myself to the kitchen to get our lunch goodies ready.

Overwhelming thankfulness fought against my jaded heart, and I didn't know if I should grab Vigil's bearded face in my hands and kiss him or order him to get the hell away from our house.

7

VIGIL

A preseason Jets game, and Michelle treated it like the Super Bowl. Dillon hadn't been lying when he'd listed the foods she always made. The nachos? To fucking die for. The chili? Spicy as fuck and so damn good I ate two bowls piled with cheddar, fresh tomatoes, and sour cream. She even pulled out wings and some sort of gooey cheese dip for the second game and kept our glasses filled with tonic and ice.

And the chocolate chip cookies ... yeah. Hanging with Dillon and his mom was going to fluff up my middle if I didn't watch it. I felt like a goddamn king on a throne even if the widow's old couch lay threadbare beneath my ass.

I thought back to Sundays spent with Ricky

watching football. Fuck, did I miss our closeness. At least he'd been around the club the rest of the week, explaining his absence at Wednesday's meeting due to his yearly check-up or some such shit. At least he wasn't getting fucked up. Seemed to be making better choices.

I glanced over at Dillon to find him piling more wings onto his plate, and grinned. He didn't know how lucky a kid he was having Michelle for a mom.

"She's a good woman, your mom," I told him quietly when the second game cut out to commercial and she'd left us for the kitchen for the tenth or so time since I'd arrived.

"Told you."

He tore into another wing like a starved caveman. She must have made four dozen, and Dillon had packed away over two on his own. "Where do you put it all, Dill?"

"Damned if I know," he replied, tossing the bone into the bowl on the stained coffee table set aside for scraps. "Wish it went straight to muscle."

"You'll get there. Keep lifting those weights."

"Plan on it—unless you're sick of seeing me over there every day."

I huffed a snort. "Nope. You're good company."

He grinned, and I rubbed a hand over my chest

as that damn ache returned. "I'm proud to call your old ass my friend, Vigil."

We laughed as I elbowed him. "Don't let your mom hear you talk like that, or she'll kick my outlaw ass to the curb before you can blink."

"Nah. I cussed before I met you, so you're good. She grumbles a lot but doesn't have real teeth to back those threats up."

I wondered—and secretly hoped she did have a set of sharp teeth on her.

Needing to take a piss, I left him alone for a few, meandering into the kitchen on my way back from the bathroom when I saw Michelle hadn't returned to the living room.

She stood at the sink washing up some dishes, her long t-shirt hiding the top of her ass, her frumpy shorts hiding the rest. Didn't keep me from sporting a chub, though.

I must have made some sort of noise, because she glanced over her shoulder, catching me checking her out. "Everything okay?"

"Better than okay," I replied, moving into the kitchen and leaning against the counter beside her, my arms crossed. "Thanks for inviting me over. It's nice to get a taste of normalcy for a change. Definitely don't get that at the club or in my empty house."

"We're hardly normal," she said under her breath, focusing on the sudsy water she submerged both hands in while scrubbing away at a pan.

"But you're attempting it for his sake. That's what's important."

She shifted her head to peer up at me, her gaze searching, probably wondering what all I knew about their secret past—which was next to nothing.

Eyes so dark they almost swallowed her pupils ... I'd never seen their likes. Hoping for a flash of sass, I smirked and dropped my attention to her lips for a second or two, just long enough to stiffen her entire body.

"Don't."

I slowly slid my gaze upward to meet her narrowed eyes. "What?"

"Look at me like that." She all but hissed the words, fire lighting in her dark orbs.

My grin widened and my dick swelled, ready for a little fun. "How's that?"

"Like you want nothing more than to order me to my knees to suck your dick."

Fuck. Me. I didn't bother holding back my groan. "You've got one hell of a mouth on you, wildcat."

She glared.

"Goddamn." I adjusted my swelling length, cursing myself for agreeing to not hit on her. "You talk like that and a man's mind starts to wander."

Michelle snorted and returned to her dishes. "As if it wasn't wandering before. You're a biker who has club whores at his beck and call ready to drop to their knees at the slightest hint of command."

"How do you know so much about biker clubs?"

She clamped her lips shut.

Quite a bit, I'm guessing. "Tell you what. I promise to never order you to your knees to suck my dick even when I'm dying to," I said, jerking her focus back up at me when she didn't reply. "Deal?"

Red flushed her face. "I wouldn't even if you *did.*"

"Hmm." I leaned back to get a better look at her body, taking my time since we'd already crossed a line of sorts—even though our banter wasn't the hitting on she said wasn't allowed. "Your hard nipples beg to differ."

"Stop looking at my breasts," she whispered harshly, yanking up the strainer from the sink.

"Can't help it. Haven't seen that lush an eyeful in—"

A pile of suds splattered in my face before I could blink. "Ow!" I laughed, swiping my forearm across my face. "That fucking burns!"

"Told you to quit looking," she grumbled, pressing a towel into my hand. "Figured you might scare off like a cat if I flicked water at you. Works on De—Dillon."

"Girl, that kind of sass only makes my dick harder," I said, making note of her near slip up while wiping the towel across my eyes. I leaned down close to her face.

Her pupils widened along with the part of her lips, and for the first time, I got a good whiff of her clean scent. All woman and clothes detergent. No flowery perfumes or cloying scents meant to lure a man in.

No, Michelle didn't need that shit. Even her lack of makeup and short, unpainted finger nails appealed to me.

"Dillon says you hiss but don't claw." I tossed the towel aside.

She glared but didn't respond—or back down.

"I love a little wildcat who won't easily bend. Turns me the fuck on, Michelle." When she didn't scoot away, I stepped in closer, trapping her against the counter with my hands on either side of her, but keeping from touching her curves in any way.

She flinched on a gasp—and not the needy kind —giving me another tell into her past. Her chest rose quickly with inhales, the pulse thrumming in her neck like mad. Pink, full lips parted, pupils wide ... fucking goosebumps rose along the arms she wrapped around herself. "Thought we had a *deal.*" Her husky, snippy as fuck voice oozed pre-cum from my dick, but I held in my groan.

No denying her body wanted me, but I wasn't an asshole who would take what she wouldn't willingly offer, especially with what her flinch had told me.

Dillon's mom had been on the receiving end of the sort of shit that boiled my blood to the point of spilling another's.

Forcing that shit from my head, I licked my lower lip real fucking slow and smirked when her breath caught. Stepping out of her space, I picked a cookie up off the plate on the table and shoved it in my mouth. A wink, an adjustment to my throbbing, leaking dick, and I left her alone.

8

MILA

*F**ucking asshole.*

I'd said no hitting on me, and while he might not consider tossing out crass compliments as such, I sure as hell did. My pissiness wasn't only from that fact. Spatting with him heightened that life simmering inside me, and I felt alive. And the fact he was amused by my snippiness rather than angry...

It took another hour before the annoyance radiating through me eased enough for me to relax. Twinges of need still zapped at me whenever our eyes met, but I narrowed my gaze every time until he turned away with a chuckle. Obviously pissiness wasn't going to rid me of his attention. I decided to go with indifference since that wouldn't "make his cock hard."

I'd gotten a close up eyeful of said cock inside his tight jeans as he'd stepped away from me in the kitchen, leaving me a soaked, trembling mess. The man was packing, and I hated the curiosity that lit me up from head to toes. Desire to drop to my knees, unzip those jeans, and find out for myself exactly what he hid in there raced my heart and made my mouth water for a taste.

Butterflies plagued me, and I told myself I hated it. Jitters swept through me whenever I felt his gaze on the side of my face. My disinterest didn't keep him from looking, but if he caught me doing the same, I simply looked away, faking the deadpan face that didn't match the wild havoc inside me.

Devon bonded with Vigil over the second game, both rooting for a team they could agree on. Pittsburgh Steelers. Other than gold and black uniforms, I didn't know jack shit about the team. The two of them talked about the players, some first and last names as though they shared childhood memories of the guys.

Vigil treated my son like a man. Called him by name, even if it wasn't his real one, never once calling him kid or punk like my ex had always done.

I might have been quick to judge Vigil, because other than the whole flirting in the kitchen episode, he didn't come across as a biker the entire afternoon. He also kept his cursing to a minimum, surprisingly. Didn't make another pass at me whenever I slipped into the kitchen for a break from the crackling tension between us, either.

When the game ended, Vigil clasped Devon's hand. "See you tomorrow, Dill?"

Devon shot a glance my way as I stood from the chair. I nodded, hating to give my consent, but not having evidence enough to forbid their friendship. "Mom's gonna give me the calories so you can show me how to put the muscle on."

Vigil ruffled his hair and laughed, sending a rush beyond longing through me. My throat thickened as Devon grinned up at him.

"You pack away food like you did today," Vigil said with a grin, his steel-like eyes warm, "and we'll have you filled out and rushing through defensive lines like a damn steamroller by next season."

He turned his intuitive eyes on me, his smirk still in place. "Thanks again for the invite."

"Anytime," I tossed out on auto pilot, and immediately snapped my mouth shut, silently cursing myself and wishing I could take it back.

His lips spread wider within his soft-looking beard, and I fisted my hands at my sides. "Gonna take you up on that, wildcat."

I forgot about indifference and glared, and he chuckled while turning to walk out the door.

Devon flopped back on the couch, and I found myself following Vigil outside.

"Hey," I called to him, shutting the door quietly behind me. He hadn't yet reached the corner of the house, and turned to face me. The streetlight lit the side of his face, but I couldn't make out his expression in the warm, quiet night around us. "Thanks for investing in my son. It hasn't been an easy transition, and it's good for him to have a friend."

"What about you, Michelle?" he asked, his low voice pebbling my nipples. "Do you need a friend?"

"What I want doesn't matter."

His gaze narrowed a bit. "That doesn't answer my question."

I studied him for a few seconds before coming up with a decent enough reply. "I don't need the kind of friend that compliments my tits, no."

"Can I point out your other fine features like your fine as fuck ass?"

Of course he would go there, the asshole. I crossed my arms and frowned, expecting he could see my face clearly in the outside light shining above the stoop. "I'd prefer if you didn't."

"Because you already know how hot you are or because you question that fact?"

"Because compliments aren't going to get your hands inside my pants," I snipped.

"What if you're wearing a skirt?"

I rolled my eyes, but couldn't bite back my smirk fast enough. Goddamn the man for making me like him. "I'm not going there, Vigil."

"I can't promise my mind won't go there," he tossed back without hesitation. "Especially in about five minutes when I attempt to take a cold shower and calm the fuck down."

I snorted, the thought of him wrapping his big hand around his cock while thinking about my *lush tits* and *fine as fuck ass* sending a rush of wetness to coat my panties for at least the tenth time that day. "Good night, Vigil."

"Good night, wildcat." He turned, but I caught the adjustment he made to his bulge trapped in those tight jeans.

Damn him.

I slammed and locked the door behind me, drawing Devon's attention off the post-game show.

"Thanks again, Mom. That was probably the most fun I've had on a game day."

My smile came easy, and I leaned down to kiss his forehead. "I start my new job tomorrow, so I'm heading to bed, baby. Don't stay up too late."

"I won't."

"Other than going to Vigil's, I want you to stick at home tomorrow, okay?"

"Yep. You already said," he replied, his focus back on the TV.

"I'll be gone before you wake up."

"Yep."

"And you've got me on speed dial—"

"Mom." He rolled his eyes.

With a heavy sigh, I turned away thinking as I did throughout every single day that my little man was growing up too damn fast and no matter what I did to protect him, I would fail.

I brushed my teeth, emptied my bladder, and crawled into bed a few minutes later, my clunking AC drowning out the sounds of the TV in the living room. Leftover energy from Vigil's presence and his words still tickled over my skin.

Between him and the new job starting the following morning, I knew I wasn't going to sleep.

I'd told myself I had zero interest in touching

myself to thoughts of even a decent man, but who was I kidding? At the least, I would sleep better.

Rather than ignore the feelings Vigil brought to life that I hadn't enjoyed in years, I focused on it and allowed the fantasy to unfold, sliding my fingers beneath the elastic of my panties. Widening my legs and a quick downward sweep lifted my hips off the bed and solidified one fact in my head.

Vigil turned me on to the point of combustion with mere words alone. I couldn't decide if I hated or loved that fact.

Lower lip between my teeth to keep quiet, I used my fingers to bring myself release I hadn't enjoyed in too damn long a time. My pulse thundered in my ears as the vivid memory of his blue-gray eyes seared through me, flushing my entire body.

My climax ripped through me, arching my back, sending a rush of wetness to coat my fingers. His name whispered in my head, but I clamped my teeth shut to keep from putting that fact into the atmosphere.

"Damn him," I whispered as my heart thudded in my ears and I came down from my pulse-thrumming high.

I told myself there was nothing wrong with a little fantasy involving a beastly ginger and his massive cock. I also told myself I would be ordering myself a vibrator the next day when I got home from work. Might as well get off on the fantasy of him since nothing would ever come of it in real life.

God knows my body sure as hell relaxed into the old mattress. Touching myself to thoughts of Vigil had been worth it. I just had to keep that fantasy in check.

I closed my eyes with a sigh and rolled to burrow into the pillow, not even bothering to force away my smile.

VIGIL

"Got anything for me, Devil?" I asked the second he walked into my office on Wednesday morning.

He pulled his laptop from the black leather bag over his shoulder and set it on the edge of my desk. "Nothing."

"You're fucking with me."

"Nope." He sat in the chair across from me and booted his laptop up. "It's like they never existed, same as I said last week."

"Witness Protection?" I asked what I'd concluded.

"Either that or they're running from something or someone and know a guy who hooked them up."

Not that it truly mattered, but Michelle and

Dillon lived in my neighborhood, and I didn't exactly like not knowing who or what I might face in the future because of their secretive past.

"They're hiding some*thing*, I know that for sure," I muttered, my fingers taking up a steady tap on my desktop like they normally did when I thought too hard.

Ryker and Stone walked in, Stone dropping onto the couch while my Sergeant at Arms leaned against the wall in his usual stance.

"Where's Ricky?" Ryker asked.

"Don't know."

His scowl mirrored mine. "Want me to go upstairs and drag his ass out of bed?"

"He's not up there," I said, my mind replaying walking into his unlocked disaster of a room a half-hour earlier—same as I'd done the week before. "Already checked. Bike's gone from out back, too."

"Two weeks in a row," Ryker said.

"Yeah. Don't know what the fuck is going on, but I will soon. Let's get started," I said, deciding to save the topic of his bullshit for later. "Devil?"

Our treasurer gave his weekly numbers report. He went on for a few about the income from the chop shop and the current black market he dealt with while I fought to focus.

Between Ricky, Dillon hanging at my place the previous two days while his mom worked, and my watching their house like a goddamn stalker in the hopes for an eyeful of the wildcat, I had a lot on my mind. As long as the shop made money atop paying Ryker, Sully, the other mechanics, and their secretary Dasia, I didn't give a fuck.

"Ryker, you talk to Klingon lately?" I asked once Devil finished up with his report.

He shook his head.

"I'll give him a call later on to see how things are going out there," I said, still distracted. "I'll ask after Jenny, too."

"Sounds good."

"Nothing new on those fuckers we helped put behind bars?" I asked about the next old bullshit we needed to keep an eye on.

Stone leaned forward, elbows on his knees. "Giada's sister said the senator is adamant on keeping the cartel members there. No plea bargains, no parole."

"That take down definitely helped her father's image—and the promise to clean up the streets even though we're the sneaky fucks who did it."

"You mean *I'm* the sneaky fucker."

I snorted at Devil. "Take the credit, I don't give a fuck. It's done, that's all I care about."

"Giada and her father make amends?" Ryker asked Stone, still unmoved from his propped up position beside my door.

"Fuck no. He wrote her off, and I wouldn't want it any other way. She sees her sister once a month without his knowing, so she's content."

"So what else is going on?" I asked, glancing from one officer to another. No one had jack shit to say. "It's too quiet."

Ryker nodded his agreement, and I sat back with a heavy exhale. "Even though we don't have any bullshit right now to keep us on high alert, I don't want to get lazy and blindsided. Let's keep our eyes and ears open. Ryker, want to put some feelers out down in Southie? Make sure there isn't new cartel or sex slave shit stirring up?"

"Will do."

"Devil, work your magic."

"I always do."

"Cocky prick," I jabbed with a grin.

"And you fucking love me," he said, snapping his laptop shut and blowing me a kiss.

"Damn right."

He stood last to follow Ryker and Stone out a few minutes later.

"Keep on digging for my new friends, yeah?"

Devil peered at me, one eyebrow raised. "You like this girl or something?"

I tipped my head to the side and shrugged. "She's one hell of a wildcat with an ass I'm dying to get my hands on."

He chuckled. "Guess that's a yes. Thought you didn't like baggage, though?"

My forehead furrowed. "Dillon's not baggage," I shot out without thought and instantly wondered over my protective nature—especially *against* one of my brothers.

Devil's eyebrow rose again, but higher. "Well I'll be damned."

I scowled and threw a pen at him. He laughed and ducked. "Just keep digging."

He nodded and disappeared out my door.

I glanced around my office, my hands lightly resting on the old desk I'd sat behind a hell of a lot longer than I'd ever expected to. We'd had a good run, my brothers and I, and having Ricky by my side as Vice President couldn't be beat. My only living relative, my only real family left on the face of the fucking earth.

Lips pursed, I considered his situation. I'd warned him to not fuck up again. So why the fuck did he skip out? Fuck knew the meetings the previous couple of years never lasted more than a half hour. Wasn't like it was laborious or dull. Hell, we'd even thrown a few punches, something he and I both enjoyed the hell out of.

I scrubbed a hand down over my face and beard, tugging on the wiry strands below my chin. "The fuck am I gonna do with you?" I muttered to no one. He claimed to be sober since the day he fought with Bucky, and I hadn't seen evidence or heard stories otherwise, so where the fuck had he gotten to?

The text I'd shot off to him at finding his room empty hadn't been answered.

Tapping my fingers on my desk, my focus on my cell, I decided to make a call. While I'd never been close with Klingon like Ryker was, I couldn't deny the man had one hell of a head on his shoulders. It was like the fucker had his masters in psychology or some such shit.

I placed the call thinking it was time for some serious change—in the hopes of *seeing* some serious changes.

My brother might hate my guts for life, but maybe he'd have a better chance at said life. Sometimes making the right choices for loved ones hurt like fucking hell, but I would do what was right for Ricky even if it tore us apart.

10

MILA

My body ached, but I supposed that was normal for working thirty hours as a janitor where there was more than enough work for one woman alone. At least I kept busy scrubbing rooms, toilets, and buffing floors, and didn't have too much frivolous down time. It didn't keep my mind busy, though, and I thought entirely too much about our situation, but more about Vigil, damn him.

I put that new vibrator to good use. Got my money's worth in forty-eight hours easily. It still felt like something was missing, namely a large cock, hands and mouth, hard muscle and cradling arms. Vigil had all of those and tempted me to just have a bit of fun. Fucking only, no attachment.

I knew myself too well, though. I craved compliments even though I pushed them away. I desired affection knowing hands oftentimes hurt. I wanted intimacy even though vulnerability scared the shit out of me.

At least I had my son who fulfilled a little of those longings.

I glanced over at Devon in the passenger seat as he fiddled with the car's radio. We'd gone out after our breakfast—my toast and his entire box of cereal—with his school supply list on our day's agenda. We hadn't been out on a date for years. When he'd been younger, we used to get ice cream every weekend and walk on the beach collecting shells and pretty stones.

Once I hooked up with the ex, going out without him or an enforcer got nixed. We had no independence and rarely any freedom.

We truly had so many things to be thankful for.

He scrolled through a station, the upbeat music that cut in and out bringing a smile to my face.

"Oh! Put it back!" I said, twirling my finger like I rewound the station.

"This stupid song?" Devon asked, settling the radio back on the One Direction song I loved.

"Yeah." I belted the chorus knowing he rolled his

eyes, loving that he let me have my time. "Nobody, nobody!" I sang with my boys.

"Mom," Devon groaned.

I sang louder, turning the volume up to drown out my lousy voice. Laughter burst from me when he slapped his hands over his ears. Carefree and easy, and I clung to that feeling hard as hell, needing that to be our new normal.

But the song ended too soon, and Devon turned the volume back down.

"Hey." He sat forward, peering out the windshield while I continued to grin. "Is that Vigil's pack?"

My heart stalled out as I focused on the biker ahead, noting the five or so others ahead of him. The old crashed into the new in the bubble I'd placed around us in those precious moments in song.

We gained on the biker group even though I left off the gas a bit, keeping with the traffic on 95 north. My GPS told me our exit veered to the right in a mile, and I gripped the steering wheel tighter.

The back of the road captain's cut became clear, the top rocker answering Devon's question.

"It's them!" Pure joy shone through my son's voice, and my stomach churned.

Their blinkers went on seconds before I hit mine

to take the exit my GPS commanded. The pack took the exit. Unfortunately, I had to as well.

They merged to go left at the light, and I pulled straight ahead toward the other waiting cars, passing the bikers one by one, their loud rumbling racing my heart. Vigil led his brothers, and I held my breath while glancing over at him.

"Mom! Window!" Devon barked, and I caved. "Vigil!" he shouted over the barking engines as the light turned green.

Vigil turned, his face lighting up in a grin when his focus landed on us. He lifted a hand to wave, and a horn sounded behind us.

I ripped my attention off the tight white t-shirt clasped around his upper arms beneath his cut and moved forward with traffic.

Devon swiveled to keep them in sight while I crossed Route 1, heading for the shopping plaza.

It took a good fifteen minutes of walking around the superstore to calm myself down. Would I ever be able to hear a chopper without anxiety twisting my stomach or fear jerking my heart into hyper-drive?

We crossed off one item after another from Devon's list, even the laptop the high school suggested he acquire. While there, I also insisted on a couple pairs of jeans and new sneakers. They weren't the best brands, but we didn't have the funds we'd used to.

At least Devon wouldn't go without.

Arms loaded with bags, we meandered back out into the bright sun. At least the humidity had pushed out of New England with the south-easterly wind fluttering strands of my hair around my face. It smelled like the ocean, and the sudden yearning to see its waves crash on the shore sent an ache through me.

"We ought to go get some lunch," I said, glancing around for the car. I'd been too upset by Vigil's pack to take note of where I'd parked.

Devon stepped ahead with confidence, so I followed on his heels. "McDonalds?" he asked.

I grimaced. "I was thinking more along the lines of—"

"Vigil!"

I side-stepped to peer around Devon and found Vigil leaning against our car, his bike parked in the spot beside it. My heart took off again, and I inhaled a steady breath before plastering a smile on my face.

Grinning again, Vigil popped the trunk that I hadn't locked.

That damn man totally discombobulated my brain. I never forgot to lock my car...

"How you doing, Dill?" he asked, after a quick glance at my face.

"We just got all my shit for school."

I started to chide my son, the name Devon on my lips. Snapping my mouth shut, I watched Vigil take his bags and put them in the trunk before slapping his back in a bro hug.

My hands shook as I put one arm load into the trunk beside the other bags.

Vigil let go of Devon and grabbed the others from me. "Wildcat," he murmured in greeting, the nickname heating my cheeks.

Refusing to give him what he wanted, I went with an indifferent tone while replying, "Vigil."

"You got my text," Devon said, snapping my head his way and narrowing my gaze even though he didn't look at me. Sneaky little turd.

"Yeah, and I was thinking about hitting the clam shack before it shut down for the summer," Vigil replied. "Figured I'd wait for you to finish shopping to see if you wanted to go with me."

Devon glanced between the two of us, the wide smile still on his face. "You wanting a date *with my mom* or the two of us?"

Vigil smirked while shoving his hands into his jean's pockets. "Wouldn't mind a date with your mom, but I'm not her type."

Devon snorted. "You're exactly her type. Red hair and all."

"Dillon!" At least I remembered the proper name while shooting daggers at him with my frown.

Vigil chuckled. "How about those fried clams?"

"Mom?" Devon's dimple popped, and I rolled my eyes.

"Fine."

My son let out a whoop and rounded the car.

"Can I offer him a ride?" Vigil asked quietly.

"No," I shot back, while rifling for my keys in my purse.

He started toward the bike. "Stick close," he said, straddling the Fat Boy. The engine roared to life before I climbed in the car, but it didn't affect me the same as the pack's noise had earlier.

"Thanks, Mom," Devon said as I backed out.

Falling in behind Vigil, I nodded, forcing another smile.

———

"Did you get your schedule?" Vigil asked Devon when I settled onto a picnic table beneath the shade of a towering pine tree.

"Yep," Devon replied around a mouthful of fries he'd shoved into his mouth the second he got his tray of food. "Going over there next week for a tour, too."

"You excited?" Vigil sat on the plank beside me, close enough his knee bumped mine.

I shifted to put some distance between our legs as he set my tray he'd insisted on carrying in front of me.

Devon sat across from us and shrugged, swallowing his mouthful before relaying. "Somewhat. I guess I'm more nervous than anything."

"You know I've got your back, right?" Vigil's tone didn't allow for argument.

"Yep."

"You have any trouble, you let me know."

That protective nature of Vigil's sent a tingle of warmth through me, softening that hard shell I kept myself locked up inside. No matter his kindness toward my son, no matter his sincerity in wanting to help him, I wouldn't lower my defenses again.

Even if thoughts of him got me off every single night.

Especially when the energy zapping between us distracted me from being vigilant.

I focused on my food and those around us while they bullshitted about the games set for the following day, who was favored, and making bets on which teams would win—the type of nonsense I tended to ignore when Devon got together with his friends.

Friends.

My chewing slowed as I considered my last conversation with Vigil about my needing a friend. The insinuation he'd tossed out and my vibrators over use tempted me to give into what he wanted. What my body obviously wanted, what I fantasized about.

Cursing the rippling heat and tension between the short distance separating our bodies, I focused on slathering every fried clam in the tartar sauce before popping them between my lips.

Regardless of staying away from him as far as the bench allowed, I still found my heart rate elevated, but in a totally different way than when we'd pulled alongside him and his brothers at the red light.

I couldn't keep the dampness from my core as hints of his soap and the scent of pure male filled my lungs with every inhale.

The two boys finished first and continued chatting without a lull. Weight training, motorcycle engines, aftermarket parts... Guy stuff. My heart softened even more toward Vigil, loving how he treated my son like a man and respected my wishes to keep the cursing to a minimum. I couldn't remember the last time a man respected me.

I eyed Vigil in my periphery, trailing my focus along the veins popping from his forearm all the way to his large hands resting on the picnic table. Calloused. Strong. Blunt nails, but nicely shaped without the snagged edges like my ex always sported. Vigil rubbed one finger along a groove in the table top, and I honed in on the action, imagining he used that soft, mindless caress on my hand. My arm. My neck.

An ache spread through my breasts, hardening my nipples, and I forced my attention on the family of four dining at the table behind Devon. I imagined they lived a normal life. Husband and wife, happily married in a peaceful, loving relationship. I imagined they cuddled and shared about their days once the two youngsters went down for bed. I bet he massaged her feet. Brushed her hair.

"Mom?"

I glanced at Devon. "Hmm?"

"You okay?"

I attempted a smile while gathering up our trash onto my tray. "Yes."

"I'll get that," Vigil said, standing.

"Thanks." I didn't look up at him while handing the tray over.

"Ready?" I asked Devon, pushing to my feet as Vigil took our trash over to the waste barrel.

"Yeah."

We started toward the car, the sun beating down on our heads, and Vigil joined us before we reached it.

"Heading home?" I asked him while pulling my keys from my purse.

"Yeah. You?"

I nodded and glanced at Devon. "Want a ride home on his bike?"

Dimples flashed as excitement filled my son's eyes. "Seriously?"

"If the offer still stands." I finally lifted my focus to find Vigil staring at me with gratitude. Appreciation. My damn heart fluttered.

"Yeah, come on, Dill. The p-pad is all yours. I got an extra helmet in the saddle bag."

My throat swelled as Devon climbed on behind Vigil, but it wasn't out of fear or real sadness. I actually trusted Vigil enough to not bother keeping up with them as they took off. We certainly weren't together as a couple, we weren't normal by any means, but he made my son happy.

11

VIGIL

A few hours after getting home from the shack, I noticed Michelle sitting on her back porch. Alone in the falling twilight. Nothing but a mug in her hands which meant she wasn't interested in company, including social media, but I didn't give a fuck.

I grabbed a beer from the fridge and went outside, instantly drawing her attention. She waved, and even though I didn't take it as an offer to join her, I sauntered across my lawn to the corner where the two met.

"Nice night." I went for small talk across her smaller backyard. Friendly and all that shit while my head went for bending her over the stoop's railing and plundering the goods she hid beneath those drab clothes.

She glanced westward at the sunset through the trees on the far side of her house, her face relaxed for a change. "At least the heat is gone."

I gestured to the stoop she sat on once she returned her focus on me. "Want company?"

She held my stare, electric energy rising between us. "Not really."

I swigged my beer while holding her gaze. "Not gonna bite you, wildcat."

She lifted a single eyebrow as though she didn't believe me.

A deep chuckle rumbled through me as my dick took interest in her sass. "Okay—so maybe I *would* bite given the chance."

"You're not gonna get that chance," Michelle muttered while twirling her mug in her hands.

"I heard that."

She rolled her eyes and scooted over, patting the top step beside her.

Grinning at how easily she unexpectedly gave into me, I moved closer and made myself at home, keeping my knee to myself since she hadn't appreciated the contact while we'd sat at the picnic table at the shack. "Whatcha drinking?"

"Vanilla chai tea." Her gaze flitted to my beer, and I lifted the sweating bottle, turning the label to face us.

Lips pursed, she returned her attention to the sunset.

"I'm not a big drinker," I said, holding the bottle in one hand between my knees. "If I'm in the mood to relax, I usually just smoke a joint."

"That was my go-to once upon a time," she admitted, her lips twitching. "Don't ever tell Dillon, though."

"Your secret is safe with me," I said with a smirk into my beer before taking a long pull. "Old Widow Betty used to live here." I glanced over the yard I had mowed for years because her son was too busy to help her out.

"Dillon said you took care of her."

"Yeah. She was a good one. Pretty much adopted me as her grandson."

"Did she make good cookies?"

I glanced over to find her gaze intent as though truly wanting to know. "Not nearly as good as yours."

"Thanks."

I slapped a hand to my chest. "Did you just accept a compliment from me?"

Her lips twitched, but she turned away. "Guess so."

A few night insects buzzed about, filling the quietness around us as I continued to grin like an idiot. I enjoyed a woman who didn't feel the need to fill the silence. Chattering like monkeys and squirrels only pissed me off and hurt my head. While I didn't like evasiveness and shutting out, I sure as hell liked a woman of few words.

Getting Michelle to open up about anything, though, had proven to be a damn challenge. But being a nosey bastard, that didn't stop me from trying.

"So, Dill seems to be doing pretty well." I went for the roundabout route.

"Yes, thank goodness." Her lips flatlined as she stared off across the back of her small lot.

"How about you?"

"Hmm?"

"How are you adjusting?"

"Good." She answered quickly without thought —a pure, fucking lie.

"Don't believe you, wildcat."

Lips pursing again, she glanced over at me.

I swigged, holding her gaze, loving how her dark eyes tried to shut me out with indifference and failed. My dick stirred a bit more, taking me to the point of discomfort.

"You can be honest," I said. "Dillon's not out here and it looks like you could stand to unload whatever is riding your shoulders."

"How can you tell?"

"Slight furrow between your brows. Hunched shoulders like a weight hangs around your neck. The sadness in your eyes."

She peered into her milky tea for a few seconds while I waited, hopeful as fuck she'd cave and give me a little insight into her past.

"There was some trouble back home that we're better off without," she finally said, her voice low enough I strained to hear her.

"Are your lives in danger?"

She hesitated before shaking her head, letting me know she didn't really believe her unspoken answer.

"Is the law after you?" I pushed for more.

She huffed a sarcastic laugh. "No."

"Didn't think so." I shifted a bit without getting any closer. "You seem the law-abiding type."

Her smile came easily as though my assessment truly amused her.

"You ever need me, just call. You know that, right?"

"Because we're a part of your clan."

Not a question, but still. "Yep." I finished off my beer. "And when I say anything, I mean *anything*."

That statement earned me another raised eyebrow, and I grinned again, loving where her mind went—exactly where I'd implied.

I held up my hand she'd been checking out while we'd eaten at the shack. A few wrist twists and wiggling of my fingers drew her attention to them again. "Protection or affection. Whatever you need, Michelle."

She wet her lower lip with the tip of her tongue before dragging her focus to my face. "How do you read my mind so damn easily, Vigil?"

I tucked loose strands of hair behind her ear, careful not to touch flesh since I'd promised not to without her permission. "Your eyes are open windows," I said, my own voice dropping as her lips parted.

Fuck, did I want to kiss her. Taste her. Devour the quick exhale she let out as the energy rippled between us, making me stiff as hell, aching, and leaking within a single heartbeat.

"Don't," she whispered, and I realized I'd twisted my fingers in her hair.

I lifted my focus to her eyes to find fear swirling with the desire neither of us could deny. Dropping my hand actually fucking hurt, and I eased back from her personal space I hadn't noticed I'd encroached upon.

"I've got too many demons," she whispered, searing my eyes with her own as though hoping I would understand what she didn't want to—or *couldn't* share.

"We all do," I said, all-too aware of my own demons and those I shared with Ricky. "It's what you do with them that counts."

"What do you do with yours?" she asked, her intense gaze popping open locks inside my soul too damn easily.

"Exorcise those fuckers. Face them and show them who's boss."

"Is that what you've done?"

I considered the shallow grave that held the biggest demon of them all, but admitting to that past sin would send her running for the fucking hills without a backward glance. I couldn't have that. "We've all made choices that sent consequences chasing after us," I finally said, taking my turn to check out the pink streaks lighting the sky to the west. "Some faster than others, some only in our nightmares."

"Any regrets?"

"A shit ton," I confessed with a half-smile, "but I wouldn't change my past. It led me to the Vipers, my brothers. Brought me to this neighborhood and you and Dill." I turned to check for a reaction and found wetness coating her eyes.

"I'm not going to push you for anything," I told her, hating to be honorable, "but I won't stop hoping, wildcat. Dill weaseled his way into my heart. I fucking adore that kid. Want to push him to grow and be the man he and you want him to be."

A tear slid down her cheek, and I clenched my hands to keep from wiping it away.

"You're good people, too," I continued, "and I'll always have your back if you need me."

"You forgot to add for *anything*," she said while biting back a smile even though her eyes shone with more tears. I got her true intent with those words even though she'd meant them as a tease—she thought I was just out to use her. Take advantage of her hot as fuck body.

"I'm serious as fuck right now." My lips stayed

flatlined. "Not saying all this shit to get between your thighs or have you drop to your knees in thanks."

The pulse pounded in her neck as she rubbed her lips together and glanced away.

"Gonna call it a night on that note," I said, somewhat pissed, standing abruptly to keep from reaching for her. "We good for tomorrow's games, my friend?"

Michelle tilted back her head and nodded up at me, those lush lips parted just enough to send both of my heads into a fucking frenzy.

"I'll bring the chips." I spun and stalked off, desperate to jerk on my aching dick.

"Thanks, Vigil."

I turned, walking backwards, deciding I didn't give a fuck if she noticed how hard she made my dick. If she did, she would also have to acknowledge my goddamn self-control and the fact a lawless biker knew how to follow fucking rules if they meant a damn to him.

Soft light from the stoop's sconce on the wall shown down on her dark hair, casting her eyes in shadow.

"See you tomorrow, wildcat." A mock salute, and I spun back around, desperate to get behind closed doors so I could empty my balls beyond her sight rather than right the fuck there so she could see what just being beside her did to me.

Doing the honorable thing sucked ass, but beyond the lust, I *wanted* to earn her trust. Her friendship, too, same as I'd done with her son without even trying.

How the hell did he get into my head so damn easily? Temptation to tell him the truth warred with my self-preservation. His sincerity fought with my jaded heart.

But he was a biker, a one-percent gang member who chose to disobey the law. Even though his club rivaled my ex's, Vigil would find what I had done to be distasteful. Disloyal, a character trait men like him hated. He'd called me good people, but he wouldn't think so if he knew the truth about what I'd done.

I watched him stalk away like a man on a mission, and I had no doubt what he planned to do. Take care of the hard cock along his right thigh. My mouth watered, and I tore my focus off his broad, hunched shoulders. Pure power, raw masculinity, and an honorable heart if I'd ever seen one.

My heart fluttered at the thought of letting go, arousal heavy enough to thrum my pulse in my ears. Damn him for being so perfect. Alluring.

With a heavily huffed exhale, I pushed up and went inside. Devon played some video game on the TV, but I didn't mind his occupying the only one in the house. I kissed him on the top of his head.

"I'm headed to bed, Dev."

"How's Vigil?" he asked without turning from the screen, his fingers flying over the controller in his hands.

I straightened and moved to his side to better see his face. "You knew he came over?"

He smirked enough his dimple popped. "Was gonna come out to join you but saw him sitting there on the stoop. I crept away real quiet so he could have you all to himself."

"Who said he wanted me all to himself?"

Devon laughed, but didn't look away from the TV while the colors from the screen flashed across his face in the lone lamp's light. "Come on, Mom. The guy is dead gone on you. Don't tell me you haven't noticed."

"What makes you think that?"

"The way he watches you. When you talk and when he probably thinks you don't notice him staring. If I had to bet—" Devon jerked sideways while his character tried to shy away from some beast with a club "—I'd say he's got a thing for your ass."

"Devon!"

"Sorry. Bum."

Heat flushed through me as I thought of Vigil staring at my backside.

"Give him a chance, Mom," Devon said when I didn't respond, his focus intent on the screen. "Just might be tons of fun."

I narrowed my gaze, hands planting on my hips. "And what would you know of *fun*? Last we spoke, you said you hadn't even gotten to second base with a girl."

His cheeks flushed beet red. "I might have gotten that far."

"Uh huh. So how do you know about the *fun* part?"

His character died, and he swore under his breath.

I let the curse go but kept my focus on his face.

He wouldn't look up at me, but fiddled with the controller. "I might have seen some stuff online," he squeaked.

God, I loved the fact my son felt confident enough in our relationship to be honest with me. "By accident?"

"Um ... no?"

I huffed a short laugh, my hands falling from my hips. "Take it easy on the porn, Dev. It'll give you high expectations. Ninety-nine percent is for the cameras and isn't even real—including all those perfect titties."

"*Mom*," he groaned and rolled his eyes.

"You promise me when you meet a girl and you're ready to experience that *fun*, you'll talk to me first. I'll get you whatever protection you need if you're too embarrassed to get it yourself. I don't need any rug rats running around your teenage feet or diseases that could hinder the rest of your life."

"Not interested yet, so cool your jets, *Mom*."

"Okay, *son*." Laughing again, I kissed the top of his head once more. "Get showered before you crawl into bed, Dev. You stink."

"Love you, too!" he shot as I ambled back down the hallway.

I read for over an hour while curled up on my double bed, imagining a red-headed, pale-eyed neighbor as the knight in chromed-out armor, riding in to save his beloved. He claimed his love with words—then claimed her body in a sunlit meadow where purple heather waved in a warm breeze. The author didn't mince words, but laid out the sex scene in vivid detail, heating me clear through.

Happily ever after, the end.

Sighing, I tossed the old paperback aside and stared at the discolored ceiling above. God, I missed having a man. My ex hadn't been affectionate, but damn, how I longed for hugs and snuggles beyond Devon's. He'd been clamming up on me the previous few months, and the lack of physical touch really did a number on my head.

Without giving it too much thought, I grabbed my cell and shot off a text.

Thank you for the company tonight, Vigil.

I chewed on the inside of my lip while waiting for him to reply.

V: **Talking to you is a pleasure**

A sigh fluttered from my chest at the thought of a man wanting to be with me for his own pleasure—outside of the physical. What man did that shit? Longing for more sent my fingers over the screen.

Me: **We should do it again sometime.**

V: **Whenever you want, wildcat. I'm all yours.**

Oh, the temptation to tell him to meet me out

there that very minute... Huffing at myself, I texted what I knew I ought to.

Me: **Sleep well, my friend.**

My cell dinged before I could set it down on the bed stand.

V: **I'll be dreaming of you.**

"Goddamn you, Frankie Capello," I grumbled, my mind revving back up to where it had been while reading.

I fished my vibrator from the bed stand and took care of business, but true satisfaction lay beyond reach. Cursing myself, cursing Vigil, cursing my entire existence that led to us meeting, I burrowed my head under my pillow and clenched my eyes shut. Sleep was a long time in coming.

––––––

Vigil wore another pair of jeans that fit his ass perfectly and outlined the bulge between his thighs when he came over the next day to watch the games with Dillon.

I kept to my room more than the living room, needing space to breathe. The scent of his soap and his mere presence stole the oxygen from my lungs, leaving me light-headed and all fluttery.

Arousal soaked two pairs of panties during the long hours of his visit, too, from nothing more than heated glances. Not one brush against me, no copping a feel while passing close in the kitchen. No suggestive words, either. He totally honored my request for not hitting on me.

What the hell was the man doing to me? I'd gone a long time without, but that hadn't ever turned me on to the point of combustion from a gentle brush over my clit before. But it wasn't just how he looked at me. The attention and affection he showed my son drew me in, too, ensnaring all the feels in my heart, damn him.

When the second game's fourth quarter started, I went out to the back porch with my tea, filling my lungs with the night air that didn't contain a hint of Vigil. Breathing came easier, but my mind couldn't be torn from thinking about him.

Those veined forearms. The large hands—calloused palms and strong fingers. Pecs that swelled his t-shirt. The hints of gold in his beard and the laughter in his eyes when he bullshitted with Devon.

Sighing, I propped my chin in my palm, my elbow resting on my knee while staring across our small backyard. A warm breeze tickled hair over my cheek and rustled the leaves of the trees to my right.

Stars hinted in the darkening sky, and someone's dog took to barking to ruin the serenity of my stolen moment.

The door squeaked open behind me, and I felt him before he spoke, jitters rousing to life in my belly.

"Can I join you?"

Same as the night before, I patted the stoop beside me, and he lowered into place, setting my nerve endings alive with little shoots of energy zinging into goosebumps.

"You're really tensed up today."

"Mmm," I agreed without looking at him and sipping my tea.

"Shoulders are damn near up to your ears."

"Yeah."

"Scoot over and I'll give you a massage," he said without a trace of sexual advancement.

I finally looked over at him to find a soft smile lifting the auburn hairs around his mouth. Full, kissable lips... Jerking my focus upward only made things worse. The light behind us lit one side of his face, sending the other into dark shadow.

Half angel, half demon.

A snort left me before I could stop it.

"What's so funny?" he asked, one of his eyebrows popping up along with a corner of his lips.

That damn mouth.

"You're an absolute contradiction," I muttered, hating that I couldn't just put him inside a box and label it, thus ending whatever I felt simmered between us.

"In what way?"

"You're a beam of light and a bastardly demon all wrapped up in..." I swept my hand through the hair as though encompassing him from head to toe.

"Wrapped up in what?" he pushed, his angelic eye twinkling with enough of the demon I squeezed my thighs together.

Scowling, I held his gaze. "I haven't decided yet."

He grinned and leaned back on his hands, casting his gaze across the yards separating our houses. His pecs swelled along with the muscles lining his shoulders, and my focus slid down over bulging biceps and those veined forearms again.

"You've got a thing for my arms and hands."

I jerked my head back toward the trees at being caught staring, my stomach fluttering like mad.

"Wildcat."

"Hmm?" I refused to turn.

"Do you need a hug?"

His soft tone, the lack of sexual suggestion again stung my eyes and tightened my throat. I shook my head.

"Look at me."

My head turned on its own as though I had no say in the damn matter over whether I wanted to obey Vigil's command or not. His lips held no trace of flirting, his eyes lacking the lust I'd been dealing with all day.

"Come here." He held out one arm in invitation, taking my tea from my hands with the other and setting it aside. "I've got two strong arms. Let me hold you and I promise to keep it platonic."

I gave into temptation like a toddler with a loving puppy, shuffling my backside close and pressing against the hardness of his chest. A shudder rippled through me, and I closed my eyes, soaking in his warmth, his strength, even as his scent flooded my senses and rushed warmth between my thighs.

Strong arms wrapped around me, tugged me sideways onto his lap, but his hands stayed firm and unmoving on my back and shoulder just like he'd promised.

Safety.

A tear escaped beneath my clenched eyelids, and I snuggled closer, my throat aching.

"I got you, wildcat."

And that's all it took. I bawled like a baby, clinging to his shirt, my face buried against the steel of his chest. Complete emotional release of the pent up fears, disappointments, and anger wet my cheeks and his shirt. Ten years of bullshit flowed out of me in crashing waves, beating against shore and dragging bits of sand-like regret away with its pull.

Vigil kept his hands in place, but one thumb caressed my shoulder in soothing rhythm. I focused on the touch until I quieted. Emotions spent, emptied, my body took notice of his virility, the hardness pressing against my thigh. My breasts grew heavy and nipples pebbled. Warmth sprang to life between my thighs, readying me for affection of a whole different sort.

The kind I couldn't allow no matter how much I ached for it.

I started to pull back, but Vigil only let me go so far. Glancing at his face ensnared me in his intense stare, and I held my breath.

"You alright?" he asked, smoothing my hair off my cheek, the roughness of his fingertips fluttering my eyelids closed again.

"Yeah."

"Want to talk about it?"

I shook my head while rubbing my lips together, fighting off the need to press them against his.

"Michelle."

My eyelids popped open, and tension strung tight between us, quieting all else in my ears but the steady thrum of my heartbeat and the one I felt beneath my hand where I still clenched at his shirt. Our hearts beat in rhythm, our breaths shared in the short distance between us.

Yearning to taste him swept over me, shivering me in the warm night.

Vigil eased me closer, pressing our chests together, mere inches spanning the distance between our mouths. His cock jerked against me, sending a rush of wetness to coat my panties. He was a beast, the likes of which I'd never seen or touched —and my body was onboard and screaming to dive in head first without thought to red flags.

His gaze dropped to my mouth, and I waited to see if he was a man of his word, my breath once more held tight inside my lungs.

"You test a man's restraint, woman." Grimacing, he adjusted me on his lap—off his erection rather than grind against me. "*Fuck.*"

That word on his lips, groaned with absolute need ... *holy hell, yes, please.*

I gulped, my heart stuttering as the precipice my will power stood atop trembled beneath my feet.

He set me aside with his large hands as though I weighed nothing more than that toddler who'd sought comfort, making the decision for me. I stared as he stood, adjusting his hard length less than an arm's distance away.

"Need to cool off, wildcat." He strode back into the house, leaving me wet, willing, and so damn alone I wanted to cry again.

Goddamn him to hell and back.

13

VIGIL

I kept my fucking distance for a week because I could only take so much. Every night she sat on that porch, and I watched her through my back window with the lights out like a sick perv, my dick twitching every time it seemed her gaze drifted my way.

Holding her had been nothing but torture. She fit in my arms like she belonged there, her sweet scent driving me fucking insane as I refrained from burying my face in her hair or filling my hands with her soft curves. Because goddamn did she have them and fuck did I want them. Around me. Under me. Cradling my dick in wet slickness.

I pussied out and spent the following Sunday at the club rather than hang with Dillon, catching shit from my brothers for not being around as much the previous couple of weeks. I'd been distracted big time, and it didn't go unnoticed. Telling them to shut the fuck up earned me a bit of peace, but I needed truth and definition so I wouldn't lose my fucking mind.

Devil hadn't learned anything new, but he felt the need to share the shit he had on my new neighbors with our brothers, Michelle being a single mom and how much I wanted her ass. Fucker almost got his nose flattened, and if not for Dasia's hugging his head to her tits to keep me from doing so, I'd have let my aggravation loose on his pretty face.

At least Ricky seemed to be sober, sipping a tonic rather than making love to a fucking bottle of JD. He had another shit excuse for missing Wednesday, but I could see the edge he rode in his eyes and decided to let things lie quiet until he detoxed fully.

Feeling somewhat settled with his whole affair, my damn head focused on Michelle fucking twenty-four-seven. Even though I emptied my balls every goddamn day, tension rode me like a bitch, open throttle and empty highway. Like she couldn't get enough. Twisted my insides right the fuck up with need to butt heads with Michelle again, get that rise out of her that made my cock ache.

Dillon stayed away, too, and I wondered if I'd fucked things up by hugging his mom. I'd texted him after his first day of school, and it took him two hours to get back to me. It'd been okay, he'd said. That was it. No hot girls, nothing to hint at his true thoughts or emotions. I got the same response on Tuesday and Wednesday. He finally showed up Thursday, and the second I saw his face, I knew he *wasn't* okay.

He lifted more reps, more weight, the set of his jaw and the determined glint in his eyes telling me more than his zipped lips.

"What's going on, Dill?" I pushed once he sat red-faced on the weight bench, sweat dripping off his chin.

"School fucking sucks ass."

"What happened?" I tossed a towel to him and leaned against my tool bench, arms crossed.

He wiped his face while continuing to scowl. "I'm a nice kid, right?"

"Damn straight."

"Friendly." He slapped the towel onto his knee and looked up at me, pain in his dark eyes. "Outgoing. I can talk to anyone. Make friends with anyone —or at least I could back home." His scowl deepened, and I waited as he glanced away as though searching for an explanation for whatever he'd yet to tell me—but I already knew where he was going. Expected it, actually.

The kid let me down when he blew out a heavy exhale and forced a grin. "I'm being a sensitive whiney bitch."

"The fuck you are," I argued. "Who did what? Tell me so I can go set their asses straight."

Dillon let out a huff of laughter. "Don't worry about it. I got this."

"I do worry—and I will. That won't fucking change, Dill."

He peered up at me, the admiration in his gaze sending my hand over my chest in that absent rub I found myself doing a lot of. I honestly worried about my ticker.

"Would it be weird if I said I was totally falling for you—in a totally bro kind of way?" he hastened to add.

I chuckled but didn't ruffle his hair like I suddenly wanted to. "Not weird at all, Dill. You're pretty kickass yourself."

He swallowed and glanced away. "Want to hold the bag while I go to town on it?"

"Sure thing." Letting whatever issue he faced go for the time being, I focused on being his friend and showing him how to land punches that would protect his skinny ass.

———

Friday night I went to the club to hang out and found Ricky sprawled unmoving on the couch in my office, eyes closed and mouth open, the stench of liquor and vomit spewed across the floor setting me off.

"The fuck, Ricky?" I hurried to his side, avoiding splattered puke and pressed my fingers to his neck. A steady pulse beat beneath, but I couldn't rouse him. "Goddamnit. Stone!" I hollered, and knowing he couldn't hear me, I yanked open my door and hollered his name again into the noisy club.

He looked up from where he sat at the table, and immediately set Giada off his lap, hurrying over to me.

I turned back into my office, Stone on my heels, scowling as he let out a stream of curses. "Not waking up?"

"No."

"Fuck—gotta call an ambulance, Vigil."

I cursed every word in the fucking book, but did as Stone suggested. Two hours later I sat in a chair beside my brother's hospital bed, scowling as he ignored me.

He'd had his stomach pumped and would be fine, but still.

"The fuck, Ricky? You've been doing good the past week."

Even though he was awake and lucid, he refused to look at me, refused to let me rouse his bitch attitude. I decided to hold my peace until he was ready, but when we got back to the club the next morning, he still refused to talk, acting like a petulant little child while stomping toward the stairs. He'd done the same thing that day after finally returning from wherever the fuck he'd been instead of in my office for our weekly meeting.

Closed mouth motherfucker. "Ricky."

My tone at least paused him at the foot of the stairs, but he didn't look at me.

I lifted my chin as my guts twisted. "It's rehab or your colors."

A few brothers sat in the club, and I felt their stare as the murmurs hushed to silence.

"Fuck you and your self-righteousness," Ricky said, all but spitting over his shoulder, his pale eyes like cold steel. "You think you're so much better than me."

I straightened, my scowl swiped away at his words. "The fuck you talking about?"

"Just leave me the fuck alone," he growled and stomped up the stairs leading to the apartments above the club.

"I'm serious, Ricky!" I shot after him, letting his stupid ass comment go. "You get your ass cleaned up or you're out, you hear me?"

"Fuck off, Frankie." He flipped me the bird, and I fucking snapped same as every time he called me by my real name with *that* tone. Sounded just like our prick of a father.

I caught up to his ass halfway up the stairs, and we fell down together, fists flying and curses spitting. He landed a couple blows, and I didn't take it easy on his ass even though he had to be feeling like shit from alcohol poisoning. Until my anger simmered to a force I could restrain, I'd busted his lip and his nose.

He lay sprawled at my feet in the middle of the club, and I loomed over him, fists clenched at my sides, my chest heaving beneath an ache so fucking bad my throat threatened to swell shut. "I'm all done with your shit, Ricky. You put your ass in rehab or leave your colors on my desk," I managed to rasp through my emotion.

I spun and stalked off, ignoring the quietness of those in the club who'd witnessed one of the lowest points in my life. The door didn't slam loud enough behind me, and the whipping wind as I tore up the road didn't soothe the ache in my heart and sore knuckles.

Never had I imagined turning my brother away. Never had I thought I would toss him out on his ass because he couldn't control his demons.

We shared the sin of murder and had buried our bastard of a father deep in the woods of Maine, but he'd never truly came to grips with the violence of our childhood and the justice we'd dished out with our teenage hands.

Tension still rode my shoulders, the type that always did after violence, and I cursed myself for not sticking around the club and making one of the whores get me off. Or, try to at least. But there was only one woman I wanted—and she didn't want me.

Cursing, I turned into my neighborhood and found another reason to lose my fucking shit.

A black sedan sat in Michelle's driveway behind her piece of shit car and a familiar looking guy with sandy blond hair knocked at her door. She opened immediately as though she'd been waiting for him, a real smile lighting up her face.

My heart fucking crashed and burned with one hell of a road rash. I sped past without acknowledging her as she glanced my way, instant jealousy raging atop the shit of the previous twelve or so hours. I barely refrained from pulling over and beating the shit out of the man who managed to wrangle a smile without wariness out of my wildcat. Michelle didn't want a man like me. She'd made that fucking clear as shit.

I thought we'd had a break through with that hug and all, but I'd stayed away and she hadn't texted.

Seeing truth of her claims of not wanting me sure as fuck hurt. Cursing my goddamn life, I gunned around the corner, intent on getting home and pumping iron until I passed the fuck out.

14

———

MILA

Marshal Pritt showed up a few minutes later than he'd told me to expect him, and real happiness at seeing a familiar face had me smiling.

The rumble of a bike faded that smile quick as hell, and Vigil sped past without looking at me. I blinked, hesitating in the doorway, my gaze trailing after him. Shoulders hunched, he looked like a man hurting or pissed off.

"Michelle?" Pritt murmured, tearing my attention off Vigil.

"Yeah, come on in."

"Hey, kid," he called to Devon who sat gaming in the living room with his back to us.

"Hey." Devon didn't turn, but I didn't have the energy to chide him for being disrespectful. Not that the marshal had ever shown much consideration for him, anyway.

"Coffee?" I asked Pritt, leading him into the kitchen where I'd been ready to pour myself a much-needed cup.

"Black."

I nodded, remembering how he took it.

Less than a minute later, I sat across from him, Devon's game in the other room annoying me enough I hollered for him to turn it down a bit.

"How is everything?" Pritt asked and took a sip of his coffee, his expression bored and his hazel-brown eyes showing a complete lack of true interest.

Why I'd been happy to see him, I suddenly couldn't remember. "Fine."

"Job okay?"

"Yep."

He nodded and glanced around the kitchen. "Making do?"

"Yep."

Again, he nodded. "Your husband is still behind bars—"

"My *ex*," I shot out, knowing I shouldn't have to remind him I'd been awarded my divorce while in their care.

"Yeah, sorry." He cleared his throat, but didn't

seem the least bit contrite over the slip. "Everything is the same as when you left. Most in jail, a few on house arrest. No one knows you're here."

I sat a little easier in my chair at the brief update, but my worries extended beyond our past. "Devon is being bullied in school," I blurted quietly, needing someone to know—someone besides me to care.

That at least earned me his complete attention, making me like him a little bit better again. "What's going on?"

"He won't say."

"Then how do you know?"

I stared at Pritt, my gaze unwavering. "You don't have any kids, do you?"

"No."

"Trust me when I say that I *know*, Marshal Pritt. A mother's intuition rarely lies."

He pursed his lips and slugged down some coffee before shrugging. "Probably just new kid in school shit. It's typical. I went through it, same as my brother. He'll be fine."

But Devon wasn't fine. He'd clammed up on me, completely shutting down and shutting me out.

My spine straightened as I glared at the one man who was supposed to have our backs. I realized we were just a job to him, a damn paycheck. I'd been quick to greet him with a smile, but it should have gone to the man who'd driven past without offering a wave like he always did when I happened to see him heading out or home. My throat tightened, and I got up from the table, dumping my coffee down the drain, wondering why Vigil hadn't stopped by in almost a week. But I hadn't reached out to him, either.

"If there's nothing else," I told the marshal without turning, "you can see yourself out. I've got shit to take care of."

He didn't reply, and I listened as he drank down the rest of his coffee. "Next time I'll just give you a call." The mug clanked onto the table.

"That works for me."

Without another word, he left, not even speaking to Devon on his way out.

Cold, law-abiding bastard. He was nothing like Vigil, a real man who actually cared about my son's well-being. Had Devon opened up to him and that's why he'd avoided us?

Chewing on the inside of my lip, I crept to the archway leading to the living room and watched my son.

He frowned at the TV, the controller in his hand jerking sideways as he fought a demon onscreen. I wondered at the demons inside him now that he no longer shared his thoughts and emotions with me. Was part of growing up letting them go? Allowing them to fight their own battles?

Not that Devon gave me the chance, but I expected I knew why he kept his lips clamped shut, and I had decided after two days to not push him. Without doubt, I knew he didn't want to worry me.

If only he knew I couldn't *not* worry. He was my life, my sole reason for living, and I would do whatever I had to in order to keep him safe.

15

———

VIGIL

I woke Sunday morning, sore as hell and feeling hungover even though I didn't have a single beer or shot the day before. I'd put in one hell of a workout, not stopping until I couldn't raise my damn arms against the heavy bag anymore.

Ryker called me while my coffee brewed with the news that Ricky had left his colors on my desk.

An ache so fucking overwhelming settled on my chest I had to lay on the kitchen floor, coffee and breakfast forgotten.

"He still there?" I rasped, my eyes clenched shut.

"No. Cleaned out his room and lit out."

"Fuck." I pinched the bridge of my nose. "Fuck."

"Had his bike strapped down in the back of his truck and everything."

Fucking tears stung my eyes, and I swallowed a few times, refusing to accept the demons whispering about being at fault in my head.

"He made his choice, Vigil."

I cleared my throat. "I know, Ryk. I know."

"What do you want me to do?"

"Let the other officers know. We'll talk about finding a new VP next week."

"No rush on that. Ricky might get his ass cleaned up and be back."

One could only hope...

I needed a fucking distraction, but Dillon never came over. I didn't get a text inviting me to watch the games with him and his mom, either.

I told myself to let it go, get over Michelle's stubborn ass keeping us from enjoying one another, but I fucking couldn't. That ache in my chest lingered, and I needed a fucking friend, even if he was a teenage kid. Feeling like a complete prick for having other motives beyond his company, I texted Dillon and told him to get his ass over to my place.

It was guy time.

He showed up right before kickoff, a little more relaxed than he'd been on Thursday when he'd opened up a little about trouble at school.

"How's it going, Dill?" I asked, taking the plate of chocolate chip cookies out of his hands.

"Alright."

"Saw your mom had company yesterday," I tossed right out, zero patience in my twisting gut.

"Yeah. Old friend."

"How good a friend?" I felt his stare on me as he followed me into the basement man cave.

"You sound jealous." His voice hinted at teasing.

I'd never been anything but honest with Dillon, and I wasn't about to start keeping shit from him. "Sure as fuck am." I dropped onto the couch, ripped the cling wrap off the plate and shoved a cookie in my mouth as he sat a cushion away.

"You got it bad for her, huh?"

"Fucking awful," I said around the cookie, watching amusement light in his dark eyes.

"You don't have anything to worry about with Pritt. She's not all that fond of him anyway."

Pritt. The name rolled around in my head as I recalled his familiar profile. My brain connected him to someone from my past.

Stacy Pritt.

I'd gone to school with that prick. His father's name stuck in my brain along with those demons I dealt with on occasion, too. We hadn't ever been friends, but I heard about him here and there over the years and I knew what he did for work.

Everything clicked into place in my head, settling my suspicions into truth. My wildcat and her son were in the Witness Protection program, under Stacy Pritt's care, and I was pretty sure I knew why. High profile cases concerning one-percenters tended to stick in a club president's head.

I couldn't recall her real name or all the details of the case out in California the year before, but Michelle Evans had every right to be wary around me. Her desire to keep Dillon away from me made complete sense, and I couldn't blame her one fucking bit.

Goddamn mother fucking cunt *of a life…*

Dillon watched me as I stretched my neck side to side, his gaze growing guarded. "You okay?"

"Yeah." I nodded, softening my features from the scowl I hadn't realized dented my face. "You?"

He answered with a nod, too, before grabbing the clicker to turn up the TV.

Lies from Michelle, I understood, but I felt like Dillon and I had bonded, that we had a real friendship. I actually fucking hurt over the fact he didn't trust me enough to tell me the truth.

Maybe if I opened up, told him my own secrets,

he would let me in. But could I give him that, knowing he would tell his mom about my past and ruin whatever chance I hoped to have with her?

Not that I'd really had a chance to begin with considering who she was, but still. I'd held onto that tiny percentage of hope...

The thought weighed heavy in my head, but I cared about the kid more than I cared about getting my dick wet—even if I craved Michelle's sass and company as much as I did her body.

"You're putting on a little weight," I began, deciding I didn't have a choice. I felt protective over Dillon and nothing, no *one* would keep me from helping him out.

Dillon flexed, checking out his arm. "Maybe a little. We don't have a scale, so I don't know for sure."

"You're definitely filling out."

He flashed a grin and grabbed the bowl of chips I'd put on the coffee table.

"I was a skinny punk when I was younger."

"Yeah?" He glanced at me while chomping away.

"Yep." I sat back and turned my focus on the TV, losing myself to memories I'd buried long ago. Memories that didn't burn nearly as bad as they used to, but still got to me if I thought on them for too long. "Me and my brother both." My throat tightened, and I waited a few seconds to get my goddamn emotions under control. "We were small and weak. Couldn't protect our mother from our bastard of a father."

Dillon stilled in my periphery. "He beat her up?"

I nodded and crossed my arms to keep from cracking my sore knuckles. "It's why I worked out like you do now. Needed to get bigger. Tougher. Needed to protect her. I eventually got my father to turn on me with his fists rather than her, but fighting back didn't do jack shit but piss him off more."

"Shit," Dillon murmured.

"Ricky and I went to the police, but they didn't give a shit since our father was one of their own."

"He's a cop?"

"Was." I finally turned my focus on Dillon. "The law refused to protect my mom, and she ended up in a cold grave way too fucking early." *Goddamn, that ache...*

Dillon didn't speak a word, simply stared, so I pressed onward, needing him to know in the hopes I would earn his trust, chances with Michelle be damned.

"I decided to take the law into my own hands."

His eyes widened slightly. "What'd you do?"

I held his gaze, steeling myself for the fall out, and let the unfiltered truth spew out even as it stirred the demons from my past—and the hurtful truth of how my brother hadn't ever escaped them. "I made a plan and talked my little brother into helping me out. We got our father drunk off his ass then beat him to death."

Dillon didn't so much as blink, and I knew then that he'd seen his fair share of violence. Michelle hadn't been able to shield him from it. "You got away with it," he whispered without a trace of fear in his eyes.

"As far as anyone knows—his fucking buddies at work included—he took off one day and never returned, leaving me and Ricky wards of the state."

"Holy fuck." He blinked but made no move to get the hell out of a murderer's basement.

"I got caught up with the Vipers in my early twenties and pulled Ricky in along with me when I found us a sponsor. They're my family now. My tribe, and I protect what's mine, Dill. You got me?" My voice broke a few times, but I didn't give a shit the kid got to see me vulnerable. I wanted the same from him.

"Yes, sir," he said, his voice quiet as he continued to hold my stare like a man.

I cleared my throat again. "So yeah, I've got it bad for your mom. Want to hold her tight and keep her from whatever shit is in your past. But this isn't all about her. I met you first, Dill, and you're like the son I never had—no fucking lie. I've got it bad for you, too—in a totally bro kinda way." I managed a grin, and the kids eyes filled with fucking tears.

"Am I a pansy ass for wanting a bro hug?" he asked, his voice small like a little kid.

"I'd say you're pretty fucking badass to not be running like a chicken shit after the secrets I just told you."

"You don't scare me, Vigil. I trust you."

"Get over here." I grabbed his arm and pulled him in, squeezing him tight with a side hug.

I missed my fucking brother.

Forcing myself to focus on the present and reminding myself I needed to let Ricky go, I ruffled Dillon's hair. "I got your back. You know that, right?"

Dillon let out a heavy breath and scooted back to his seat, grabbing up the bowl of chips again. He turned his focus back on the TV, and I let him go. He kept his silence, though, over both his true past and whatever at school bugged him.

Respect for his obeying the Witness Protection marshals and annoyance over his not allowing me to protect him swirled in an ugly brew inside me, but I made myself appreciate the fact he hadn't lit out. At least I had that. The future with his mom remained to be seen.

16

MILA

Vigil hadn't been outside at night all week long. Lights shone in his windows as I sat on the stoop whenever the weather allowed, sipping my tea and lonely for company, but I didn't reach out to him once. I must have reasoned wrong about him, and I told myself I was better off without a man who wasn't interested in friendship if the woman wasn't putting out.

I'd had a shit day straight from the pits of hell, though, and longing for his ear, the comfort of his arms tempted me past the point of caring he only wanted sex—even when he said he didn't.

Grumbling, I closed my eyes and let out a heavy breath.

Devon had come home with a bruise on his

cheek and waved it off with lies about falling. I pushed, and he shut down even more, slamming his bedroom door in my face. He stayed there, skipping dinner and telling me to leave him alone.

Worse and even more worrisome, I got a call from Marshal Pritt while washing up my dinner dishes. Two of my ex's men on house arrest had disappeared. Taken out by their rivals for the deeds they'd done to land them in jail? Escaped and intent on hunting down the ones who'd helped put their brothers behind bars?

The latter chilled me clear through.

Sitting out on my porch all alone probably wasn't the smartest thing to do, but it wasn't like they'd get to New England within three hours. Pritt assured me we were safe, but I felt far from it.

Anger and fear held my stomach hostage, creating a panicked thickness in my throat no amount of tea soothed. Someone had hurt my son, and no amount of self-preservation instinct would stop me from protecting him from the one threat closer to home.

I pulled my cell from my pocket and texted Vigil.

Dillon came home with a bruise on his face.

I expected to see him storm across the yards separating us, but my phone rang instead.

"The fuck?" he growled, his voice sounding exhausted.

"I don't know." I swallowed. "He won't tell me anything."

"Fuck."

I chewed on the inside of my lip, waiting.

"Sorry." Vigil grunted after a few seconds of silence over the line. "I've had one hell of a fucking day ... is Dillon okay?"

"He shut himself in his room and won't come out."

Vigil let out a string of curses. "Did he say who did it?"

"He said he tripped and fell."

"Bullshit."

"Yep," I didn't hesitate to agree.

"Want me to come over and make him talk?"

I considered the idea, but pushed it aside while staring into my tea. "That might only piss him off more. I want him to open up in his own time. It's just hard, you know?"

"What else is bothering you?"

My shoulders slumped beneath the light sweater I'd thrown on. "How can you tell, Vigil?"

"Your voice is as easy to read as your face, wildcat. Need a hug?"

More than anything.

I swallowed back the need to tell him the truth, to open up to him like Dillon refused to do with me. "Why'd you have a bad day?" I asked, diverting so damn obviously my face grew hot.

Vigil let out a heavy sigh, and I imagined him tugging on his beard as I'd seen him do a time or two. "My brother is an alcoholic, and I gave him the ultimatum of rehab or handing in his colors."

Unsure what to say at his surprising candidness, I kept quiet.

"He left his cut on my desk. Fucking took off for who the fuck knows where."

Vigil's voice broke, and an ache swept through my chest.

"I'm sorry," I offered the only thing I could, floored that he'd told me such personal information. Harlon, my ex, hadn't ever shared jack shit—club-wise or not.

"Yeah. Fucking sucks balls."

"Sometimes, you have to draw the line, Vigil. You're doing the right thing for him."

He let out another heavy sigh in my ear. "Yeah, but it hurts. We've had each other's backs since we were little, and I feel like I'm turning mine on him now."

My eyes stung. "You're not. He'll see that someday."

"So what should we do about Dillon?" Vigil's turn to divert, and I let it slide, honing in on what he'd said and how it warmed me through.

"*We?*"

"If you want my help, yeah."

"Why wouldn't I?"

Vigil's silence roused my nosiness.

"Because I think you're a lawless biker who might be a bad influence on my son?" I suggested what I'd all but outright declared the first time I spoke to him.

"Something like that," he replied, his tone guarded.

I thought again of Marshal Pritt and how he couldn't hold a candle to Vigil. "You're the only friend Devon has right now—the only friend *I* have."

"Then let me in, Michelle. Tell me everything. Tell me what I can do to help protect you both."

I opened my mouth and snapped it shut as I realized my slip over my son's name—and Vigil's not pointing it out. "I-I'll call you in the morning."

"Promise?"

I swallowed a rush of nausea. "Yeah."

My hands shook, sloshing tea over the rim as I hung up. The Vipers hated the Demented Demons MC with a violence I'd witnessed first-hand years earlier not long after meeting my ex-husband.

Had Vigil known who we were all along? Had he tried to get in my and Dillon's heads to exact revenge for his Vegas brothers the Demons had taken out? Eight years wasn't a long enough time for memories to get buried.

I slipped inside and locked the door behind me, moving from window to window to double check our safety. My heart warred with my mind as I considered the man who'd burrowed into both without my realizing it.

Sleep eluded me, but I finally came to a conclusion long into the night. I didn't doubt Vigil's caring for Devon. I didn't doubt his desire for me. The only thing I could doubt, what my jaded heart demanded was his motives for wanting to spend time with us. His true intentions. Cold hearted bastards would use anything and anyone to get their end result—including those who trusted them the most.

Memories of what he'd told me concerning his brother, though, refuted that last thought. My gut told me Vigil was a good man, and nothing in his actions or words in the previous weeks since we'd met had raised a single red flag.

With nothing left but the need to trust *something*, I went with my gut.

Devon made an appearance the next morning for breakfast, exactly as I'd expected since he'd missed dinner. I'd decided to keep the truth about the Demons who'd escaped house arrest to myself, trusting Witness Protection to keep us safe from harm as they'd done with all those in their charge since the program began.

No one had been hurt, and running off on my own wouldn't be any safer.

"You okay?" I asked as Devon fished the last bits of cereal from the milk in his bowl.

"Fine."

I eyed his scowl and the bruise beneath his eye that appeared more purple than red. "Why don't you head over to Vigil's this morning? Work off some of your pissiness on the weights and bags?"

He eyed me while lifting the bowl to slurp down the milk.

"What? You think I want to put up with your moody ass all day today? I didn't sleep worth a shit because you're lying to me, and my head is throbbing like hell."

His smirk didn't quite pop his dimple, but my heart melted all the same. "Language, Mom."

I scowled at him although I knew it didn't show in my eyes. "Get your ass out of this house and don't come back until you've gotten this shit out of your system."

Chuckling, he got up, tossed his empty bowl in the sink, and sauntered back down the hallway.

I didn't bother hollering after him to shower first. Hopefully, he'd be sweating his ass off and spilling his guts to Vigil.

17

VIGIL

No call came through from Michelle like she'd promised, and I wondered if she knew she'd slipped on the phone the night before. I hadn't corrected the name she'd called her son, but I also hadn't acted as though I'd noticed. *Had* she realized and figured that I knew the truth? Did she fear me?

The Demons and Vipers had battled for a couple of decades, so I couldn't see how she would think me or my brothers would ever harm her. She had been the key witness in the trial that ended our rivalry once and for all.

The Demented Demons MC had been dismantled from the inside out—all because of their Sergeant at Arm's old lady—Mila Zeigler, Devil had gotten the scoop for me—and her agreeing to gather inside evidence for leniency. Guess she wasn't as law-abiding as I'd thought, the little wildcat. Not outright breaking the law in my eyes, but aiding and abetting was the same to the fucking FBI.

Dillon showed up at my back slider at the same time I'd reached my patience limit, ready to storm their house and find out what the fuck was up once and for all.

"How are you, Dill?"

He shrugged but made no move to step in when I moved back and motioned him inside. "Mind if I hit the weights this morning?"

"Help yourself. Was just going to head out there myself," I lied, eyeing the bruise under his eye.

"Cool." He nodded and hopped off my stoop, obviously intending to walk around the house than through. "See you in there."

He held his silence for a good ten minutes while I spotted him bench pressing. "What's Vigil short for?" he asked out of the blue.

"Vigilante."

"As in justice?"

I nodded, and he laid back down for another set.

"I introduced myself to a few of the guys on the football team hoping to make some friends, you know?" He sat up without finishing his reps, his shoulders hunched. "Find my way into their group for next year."

I rounded the bench to stand beside him, needing to see his face.

The muscle in his jaw ticked as he clamped his mouth shut, but I wasn't having that shit. I'd promised to help him and I *wanted* to. Fucking needed it.

"They give you trouble?" I asked even though he sported the answer in a purple bruise beneath his left eye.

A tiny nod was all the answer I got out of him, though.

"That Walsh prick leading them?"

Dillon glanced down at his hands and inspected the palms, eventually creating fists. "He's the biggest fucking bully I've ever met. Thinks he owns the goddamn school because he's the star quarterback. He's big as fuck—twice my size."

"And ugly as shit," I tossed out, the desire to burn something to the ground creating a fire inside me as he lifted his focus to me, a smirk on his lips.

"Got that right."

"He the one who did that?" I asked, motioning toward his face with my chin.

Dillon let out a heavy exhale, his shoulders

finally slumping beneath the weight of his teenage world. "Yeah, and he also let me know, in no uncertain terms, I wouldn't make the team next year. He called me a pansy-assed little bitch, a pretty boy twig who would be better off dressing up like a drag queen and making a name for myself on social media instead."

Fuck, that fire burned bright, and I wanted to ask a million questions, get to the bottom of who all was involved in fucking with his emotions. I knew what I needed to take care of business, though. No sense in dragging Dillon—Devon—through the shit he'd experienced at the hands of a bully.

Fuck knew once was enough.

That punk Walsh's father had been on the receiving end of my fists years earlier, and bad blood still lingered between us, all because he'd run a stop sign and almost took out two of my brothers on their bikes.

"Just stay the fuck away from him, Dill," I said, my tone hinting at violence even though I tried to hide the ugliness rolling around in my gut. "Ignore his ass. Keep lifting and eating healthy shit. You've got a year to get where you want, and I'm going to help get you there. Understand?"

A small smile lifted a corner of his lips as he nodded. "Yeah."

"You got this, brother."

His lips stretched into a full-on grin, sending that ache through my chest again, and I clasped his shoulder tight. Emotion, not a fucking heart tick ran through my chest. I felt hurt and happiness at the same time. Best fucking feeling in the world.

"Finish up this set, then it's onto the bag. Gonna work your ass hard today."

"Bring it."

His grin eased me a bit, and the simple **Thank you** text that came through to my cell an hour or so after I sent his spent ass home made things almost right in the world.

But there were still some things that needed put straight. I couldn't do anything about the Michelle/Mila situation until she let me in, but taking care of those punk bullies I could make happen in my own time.

Devil had some digging to do first, though, since I wasn't about to take a step, guns blazing, without preparing first.

I wondered over Dillon asking me about my road name and the fact he'd spilled his damn guts right after learning I took the law into my own hands. Did he hope I would do something about his situation? He had to know I would—and I did.

———

The next afternoon, Ryker, Stone, and Warden had my back as I walked up to the Walsh's front door like I owned their goddamn mansion. Sure, he had money, but he had no connections to protect him from the *real* law in town.

I fucking missed having Ricky at my side, but there was no room for emotions on that day. Locking that shit up tight in my heart, I knocked on the Walsh's front door.

His face paled when he pulled it open.

"Your punk ass son around, Walsh?"

He straightened and had the balls to cross his arms and attempt to look down his nose at me even though the pallor of his skin revealed the quaking inside his guts. "What do you want with Ryan?"

"I don't want a goddamn thing with him other than a few words," I said, my voice laced with venom. A lie, but I'd already set up a shit storm to go into play for the kid if things didn't go my way.

Walsh glanced at my brothers behind me as

though weighing his chances of standing up to us and surviving. "What'd he do?"

"Picked on the wrong kid."

"Goddamn it." Lips pursed, Walsh shook his head as though pissed, surprising the fuck out of me. "Light into him all you want with words and set him straight for me, Capello, but if you so much as touch a hair on his head, I'll bury you myself."

"Like you tried to do once before?" I snorted, trying like fuck to keep my surprise over his demand off my face.

A muscle ticked in his jaw as red flushed his cheeks. "Ry!" he hollered over his shoulder.

"What?" the punk shot back from somewhere in the house with annoyance and complete disrespect in his voice.

"You've got company!"

Ryan made it halfway down the stairs before lifting his head and catching sight of us. His feet stalled out and he glanced at his father, licking his lips like we dried his mouth the fuck out. "What's going on, Dad?"

"Frank Capello here wishes to have a word." Walsh motioned him down the stairs, and Ryan started moving again, hesitant and wary as fuck.

"Dillon Evans," I shot out as he stood beside his

father, unable to hold my gaze even though we stood eye to eye, the pansy-assed fucking *twig*.

"What about him?" Ryan grumbled.

"He and his mother are under our protection. You fuck with him, you fuck with us."

The punk gulped.

"You bullying that boy?" his father asked, his scowl almost as deep as mine felt grooving my forehead.

Ryan opened his mouth, but snapped it shut without attempting to defend himself.

Not so big a man now, cocksucker, are you?

"Why don't you tell dear old dad here about the black eye Dillon is sporting," I growled, crossing my arms and glaring even though he wouldn't look at me.

"Ryan Williams Walsh the third!" his father snipped, fire in his voice.

Ryan looked at his father, alright, nearly pissing himself, the pussy *fuck*.

"I'm about tired of you tarnishing our name and bailing your ass out, son," Walsh hissed. "One fucking thing after another." He shook his head, and his son at least lowered his gaze. "Get the fuck back up to your room, Ry, before I let Vigil and his brothers here loose on your ass like you deserve.

And you can forget about that party tomorrow night!"

Ryan turned without a word, moving a hell of a lot faster up the stairs than he'd descended.

"You so much as speak a goddamn word to Dillon," I shot out after him, "you and all the rest of your little band of brothers, and you'll be wishing you'd only miss a party."

"Get the fuck upstairs," his dad barked as Ryan tripped, and the punk obeyed like the devil himself jabbed his backside with a pitchfork.

Walsh turned back toward me, losing the frown and the haughty stance. "He's been on the wrong path for some time. Seems he and his friends are testing the waters to see how much shit they can get away with. School called me twice this week threatening to expel him if I didn't straighten him out. He obviously doesn't respect my ass—hopefully you just put the fear of God in him."

I hadn't gone to Walsh's home to do him any favors, but as long as Ryan and his friends left Dillon alone, Walsh could think whatever the fuck he wanted.

I leaned closer, keeping my eyes hard as fuck. Unwavering. "I know about Becca Lamont."

Walsh paled again.

"There isn't much that goes on in this town we don't know about," I told him, keeping my voice low. "I had a little chat with her this morning—her *and* her parents—but they don't want any trouble since she managed to survive that botched abortion you paid for."

Walsh blinked, without doubt wondering how the fuck I knew.

It paid to have an IT hacker geek as an officer.

"I set a few things into motion to take Ryan down, Walsh. Him and his little band of gang-banging brothers." Ryker growled under his breath behind me, but Walsh held my stare, gaining a shred of respect from me atop how he'd handled my words to his son. "He escaped the law because of your money and name, but I don't give a shit about either."

"What do you want, Capello?" his voice betrayed anxiety—and the need to shit his pants.

"I want him and his buddies' dicks sawed off and burned in front of them, but I can't do that, can I?"

The air left Walsh in a rush.

"He fucks up again, and it all comes out. The extortion with her family. The entire cover up. The money you paid to keep the doctors, the lawyers, and that goddamn judge quiet. Feel me? I won't hesitate to spill your family's sin to the world. This is the only warning you'll get, Walsh."

He swallowed thickly and nodded. "Understood."

I nodded and turned without a word, somewhat disappointed I didn't get to smash a nose or two. My nerves rode a straight edge, and I needed to fucking let loose—or get laid. The thought of one of the whores at the club couldn't even get my dick hard anymore. Only one woman managed that, but I felt that whole situation was on hold until she got her shit straightened out.

"Should have fucking burned him to the ground," Ryker muttered the second we all climbed into Stone's truck. "Fucking rapist."

"He'll pay," I said, glancing over at Warden who nodded. "But it's going to look like a tragic accident."

"Too fucking easy," Ryker argued, and while I had to agree with what spurred his thoughts in that vein, I had to protect our club.

Warden had hitmen contacts at his disposal—or rather his old lady, heiress to an old cartel's estate, did. Shaun's father might have passed on, but a few of the men who'd been loyal to him still checked in on her from time to time.

Warden had already made the calls to make an

accident appear just that, same as how another cartel had taken out Giada's little brother. It fucking paid to have sneaky fuckers in your pocket—but even more so to exact it vigilante style rather than cold-blooded murder.

Justice for Becca Lamont.

18

MILA

Devon's stress and pissiness disappeared after talking to Vigil. Whatever he'd told my son, whatever encouragement he gave while working out in his garage gym, helped. While he appeared nervous readying for school the following Monday, Devon didn't drag his feet when I dropped him off. He turned and waved before I drove off to head to work, setting my mind at ease.

He hadn't shared with me, but I expected he'd spilled to a man he considered a friend, one he trusted more than his own mother. I had to remind myself he hid the truth to keep me from worrying, not because he didn't trust me.

Vigil didn't make an attempt to see me, and he didn't return my thank you text from Saturday, either. I wondered over what went on in his head while buffing the retirement home's floors, but decided to let things lie. I had enough to worry about.

The escaped Demons hadn't been found, but Marshal Pritt had called me twice over the weekend, along with his supervisor to assure me we were safe.

"How'd school go?" I asked the second I walked in our front door and Devon turned from his gaming on the living room couch.

"Good."

"Good?" My eyebrows shot up.

"Yeah. Made a new friend and everything." He tossed aside his controller even though the game hadn't ended, so I dropped my purse and sat on the chair, angling to face him.

He told me everything—from the bullying words that built up over the first week of school to the fight on Friday that resulted in his black eye.

"But they ignored me today, Mom. Didn't so much as look at me."

"Grew bored and moved onto the next victim?"

Lips flatlined, Devon shook his head. "They ignored me—like flat out intentionally didn't look at me. Almost ... almost like they were scared to."

My mind chewed on that information for a few seconds.

"Something happened." He held my gaze, and I knew.

"You told Vigil everything you just told me, didn't you?"

"Yeah."

I nodded and forced a smile. "Well, hopefully, they'll continue to ignore you and life can go on. Did you get a snack?" I hurried into the kitchen, hoping like hell Devon didn't catch the itch clawing at my skin.

"Yeah!"

I noted the bowl in the sink and empty cereal box on the counter. That kid…

"So tell me about this new friend you made," I said when I heard him follow me into the kitchen and pull open the fridge.

"He's a nerd. Total geek in the chess and technology club."

"Does he like football?"

"Nah." Devon rummaged in the fridge while I washed out his bowl. "He likes to game but he's going to give football a try, though. I'm heading over there Sunday if that's okay with you."

"Absolutely."

Good. A new friend, one who wasn't a violent biker, the neighbor I needed to have a little chat with.

"I'm running over to Vigil's real quick," I said while drying my hands off.

Devon's face broke out into a grin, and I rolled my eyes.

"Not for what you're thinking, you little turd. Just want to talk to him is all."

"Uh huh."

"Lock the door behind me."

I strode out onto the stoop, Devon's, "Have fun!" following me out.

If only.

Steeling myself with a few deep breaths, I made my way across his larger lawn, and he pulled open the slider off his back deck before I even climbed the two stairs leading up to it.

"To what do I owe this pleasure?" he asked, a smirk twitching his lips. My lack of jovial response flatlined his mouth, and he waved me inside. "Dill okay?"

"Yeah, better than okay, actually." I turned to face him once inside his living room and cross my arms as he slid the slider shut, trying like hell to block out the scent of him that permeated the cool air.

"Glad to hear it."

"I'll bet you are," I snipped, my gaze narrowing even further as Vigil stepped close rather than sit like I'd hoped for, his intense gaze searching my face. I wanted to ask about his brother. Wanted to make sure Vigil was doing okay, but I wasn't there for a friendly little chat.

"What's on your mind, wildcat?"

"I know what you did."

"What's that?" he asked without a hint of emotion twitching his face.

"You confronted those boys, didn't you?"

"Ryan Walsh and his father to be exact," he didn't hesitate in answering.

I knew it. Straightening, I held his stare. "I think it's time for you to end your friendship with my son."

"Why? Because I'm looking out for him?"

"Because you used intimidation tactics—if not violence—to do so!"

His eyes burned like molten steel, sending a shiver over me, but I wouldn't back down. "I'm sure *Devon* has seen his fair share, but at least this time it was for his benefit."

My insides quaked even as my feet rooted deep to his floor. "You don't know what you're talking about," I said, my voice having lost its solidity.

"Don't I, Mila?"

The blood rushed in retreat from my face, and I shivered. "Don't *ever* call me that. Don't ever talk to me again," I managed to spew. "Stay away from me and my son, or I swear to God..."

Feeling returned to my feet, and I fled like the gates of hell burst forth at my back.

19

VIGIL

I honored Mila's request and stayed the fuck away. Between that and me worrying over Ricky had me popping antacids like candy. Fucking stress. Devil dug into all things Demons, giving me the goods on Mila Zeigler along with her son Devon who'd disappeared after trial.

The whole affair had transpired exactly as I'd recalled, and I told my officers I had every intention of watching over them regardless of the program assigned to protect them. Stacy Pritt was a selfish bastard, and I didn't trust him to do more than the bare minimum to earn his pay. He'd been a lazy prick as a kid, too. Same as his goddamn father, the Chief of Police at the time of my mother's death.

Knowing I had my Viper brothers at my back with both the Zeiglers and Ricky shit should have set my mind at ease, but didn't.

Devon snuck over and used my weights after school while she was still at work every day that week. He told me she was being a miserable bitch and wanted *me* to do something about it, the hint in his tone coming through loud and clear.

"Thanks for your blessing, Dill," I said with a laugh, "but she doesn't want anything to do with me."

"She forbade me from coming over here."

"And for good reason."

"In her mind, yeah, but she isn't using her damn brain properly."

I set the dumbbells I'd been curling with onto the rack and turned to face Devon slouching on the bench.

"She told me that you know everything," he said, his face questioning even though he hadn't asked one.

"Yeah, but I'd already figured it out for myself."

"How?"

"I know Stacy Pritt. Know what he does, and caught both of you slipping while lying. I'm also well aware of the trial out in California last year. Didn't take much to put it all together."

Devon slumped further, averting his gaze. "I'm sorry for lying to you while you've been nothing but honest—especially seeing as how you trusted me with the shit from *your* past."

"You were protecting your mom, Dill. Nothing nobler than that."

"It's Devon."

I chuckled and tossed him a towel to mop up the sweat lining his brow. "I know. Kinda fond of your nickname, though."

"Me, too." He grinned. "We good?"

"Always."

"I made a new friend," Devon went on a short time later as though not a goddamn thing had changed between us. "Going over to his house on Sunday to watch the games."

Although bummed out, I smiled, truly happy he'd done so. "Guess I'll head over to the club, then."

"You could always keep my mom company." He waggled his eyebrows, and I snorted a laugh.

"She won't let me in the door."

"Doesn't hurt to try."

His words burned through me, and with Ricky's

location still a mystery, by Sunday, I'd had enough. I needed some fucking closure in one way or another, and Mila lay less than a hundred yards away.

I knocked and waited, not bothering to hold my breath. Needing *something*, I knocked again. Harder. "Come on, wildcat," I growled, knocking a third time.

She wrenched the door open, ripping the breath from my chest. Hair dripping, a towel wrapped around her body, she glared at me with dark, flashing eyes.

"I was in the tub. What do you want?" she spat.

I cleared my throat and forced my focus on her face rather than the swell of her breasts I'd never gotten a good look at. "Can we talk?"

"I've got nothing to say to you."

A muscle ticked in my jaw, and I stepped forward, being the bully she wanted to believe me to be.

"What are you doing?" she asked, scuttling back a few feet and grasping her towel tight against her chest with two hands.

I shut the door and turned toward her, my face and eyes unshielded and open for her to read whatever the fuck she wished.

She licked her lower lip and glanced away, a shiver pebbling her skin.

The drive to dominate, take what we both wanted rushed through me, and I stepped forward, running my fingers through her soaked hair.

"Stop touching me."

"No," I tossed back, so damn done with her shit.

"I hate you."

"No you don't, wildcat. You hate the *idea* of me." I dropped my hand and fisted them both at my sides to keep from yanking her into me. "Or rather, that preconceived notion in your head that I'm like the asshole who did you wrong."

"You *are* like him."

I moved in, and she stepped back, both of us not stopping until the wall hit her back. "Look me in the eye and tell me that, Mila."

She lifted her face with a stubborn tilt, pissiness in her eyes, sure, but pure fucking lust as well.

"Gonna kiss you, wildcat," I warned her, my gaze dropping to her lush mouth.

"No."

I grinned and leaned in close enough to breathe in her sweet, panted exhales. "Yes."

"Damn you, Vigil," she moaned, her husky voice betraying her.

"Give me permission, wildcat."

"No." She shook her head even though her dark eyes with their blown out pupils wouldn't look away from mine.

"Mila."

One whimper—and she scaled up my body like a goddamn monkey, plastering her mouth to mine. Took me all of one stuttered heartbeat of mind-blown fuckery to respond. My hands grasped her ass and I pressed forward, slamming her back against the wall, taking control of a kiss she thought to take from me before I stole it from her.

Her tongue begged entry, and I let her have it, groaning as her sweet taste filled my mouth. Goddamn, the hunger ... grasping hands at my hair and shoulders, moans and whimpers escaping her into my mouth, and her squirming body, fucking lush curves grinding against me.

I dug my fingers into the flesh of her thighs, hitching her higher and settling her against my aching dick. The towel sagged to her waist, and I ripped it away, grinding against her core.

"I don't want this," she whined against my mouth while rubbing herself all over my jeans.

I shoved a hand between us to cup her pussy and damn near lost it at the slick wetness coating my palm. "Stop lying to me, wildcat. Your dripping pussy says otherwise."

"Goddamn you, Vigil."

"My soul is already damned. I need someone to save the rest of me."

20

MILA

His words echoed in my head as he claimed my mouth, and my body melted into him, needing more. So much more.

"Vigil," I whispered against his mouth, and he pressed two fingers deep inside my emptiness, the rough pads of those tips finding what no man had before. "Oh, God." I tore my mouth from his and tipped my head back, gasping for breath as he played me like a fine harp and him the master of its strings.

He latched onto my neck, the springy hairs of his beard soft yet abrasive, sending tingles across my skin and tightening every muscle in my body. "Fuck, wildcat." He pumped his fingers slowly in and out of my sopping core while tasting every inch of my neck, lifting me higher with the hand beneath my ass to get to my breasts.

"Fuck," he muttered again, burying his face in my chest, lips, tongue, and teeth making themselves right at home. His thumb found my clit and teeth clasped over my aching nipple.

"God." I clasped his head, holding him right *there*. Right, fucking *there*. My breath caught—and I came hard as hell, creaming all over his fingers, jerking in his hold, his name panting from my parched mouth.

"Vigil," I breathed, and he lifted his head, taking my mouth again, grinding away against the back of his hand still rubbing at my core.

I came again, crying out my release in his mouth, and he groaned, drinking down every whimper, soothing every shudder that rippled over me while coming down. He trapped me against the wall with his hips while pushing my wet hair back and cradling my face with one hand.

Lust still shone from his pale eyes, but more resided beyond. Enough it scared the shit out of me. He slowly sucked his fingers clean then kissed me gently, and goddamn my own soul, I couldn't keep from responding regardless of the tangy taste of me on his tongue.

"I don't want this," I said against his mouth, my eyelids screwed shut so damn hard I frowned.

"Then stop kissing me. Stop touching me."

"I can't." I pulled back to find my hands still threaded in his hair as he continued to cradle my face in his calloused, gentle palms.

"I'm not him."

Tears welled in my eyes, and I couldn't find my voice.

"I'm not him, Mila."

"I know," I managed, and a tear slid down my cheek. He licked the salty droplet, and another shudder rippled through me, sagging me against his rock hard body.

"Give me a chance to prove it." He brushed his lips over mine even though lust had him hard as steel between my thighs. "Give me a chance to earn your trust." Burying his face in my neck, he found my sensitive flesh with his hand again.

"I don't just want this pussy—I've always wanted more. From the first time I saw you, I *needed* more."

Goddamn him to hell and back.

I loosened my hold on his hair and wiggled until he set me on my feet.

"Mila?" Vigil stepped back, giving me the space I needed, and I wrapped my arms around my chest.

He grabbed my towel and handed it to me, pausing when his gaze slipped to the apex of my thighs. "You're a blonde."

I snatched the towel and wrapped it around me with trembling hands while his focus flitted up to the dark hair atop my head. "Yes, I'm really blonde," I snapped as he frowned. "I've lied about a lot of things."

"I know the truth." He met my stare head on. "And I understand why you lied, but no more, Mila. If you keep hiding shit from me, I can't protect you."

"It's not your job." I scuttled around him, heading for the door.

"It is," he argued, his tone not inviting a contrary response, but I didn't give a shit.

"What the hell makes you think it is?" I shot back, grasping the door's knob.

"Because you're mine."

Fire raced through me, and *so* not the kind he probably hoped for. I fucking snapped, shooting daggers over my shoulder at him. "*The hell I am.*" I yanked open the door. "I belong to no man, Frankie Capello. I won't be a possession. Won't allow a biker asshole to hurt me or my son ever again. Get. Out. And stay away from us."

He stared at me, hands fisted at his sides, his

cock still hard and alongside his thigh—unfinished and hopefully aching if the wet spot at the head was any indication.

I hated that drool flooded my mouth.

"Out," I snapped again, stomping my foot and pointing into the night. "Now."

Vigil's glaze slowly slid over my face as though memorizing every line, every hint of wrinkle that had made an appearance in the previous year. "I'll always honor your requests, wildcat." He walked past me, and I slammed the door behind him with finality.

Tears welled in my eyes, but I bit my lip to keep the rising sob suppressed. My emotions sucked at my sanity like an undertow, and I made it to my bed before giving up the fight.

21

VIGIL

Mila managed to keep Devon away, and I felt like my thumb got lobbed off. That damn ache from losing Ricky intensified, and I couldn't fucking deal. The taste of Mila lingered in my memory, the scent of her coating my nose all damn week long.

Couldn't fucking sleep.

Couldn't fucking find my brother.

Not a single brother, old lady, or club whore had any hint of where he'd run off to. I called the other chapters across the country, informing them of his disappearance. Klingon out in Vegas suggested reporting him missing to the authorities.

He didn't know me well enough to know what I

thought of the fuzz and their holier than thou attitudes.

The only satisfaction I gained in that week was the story making all the local news stations. Seemed a couple football players from the high school down the road had been out partying and wrapped their car around the tree. All five occupants died upon impact. Too damn easy a way to go—I had to agree with Ryker, but there was no possible way for the accident to lead back to us.

While the town mourned their loss, I watched the Zeigler household like a fucking hawk. Turned out Mila had kept something else from me besides just her son. Two of the Demons on house arrest had taken off according to Devil, and hadn't been found.

I wondered why Pritt or one of his guys didn't watch the house. I wondered why Mila didn't just take off on her own. Did she believe the fucker could actually keep them safe?

Smoking a joint became a nightly ritual, but I still fell asleep with a full mind and an aching heart.

Mila Zeigler fucking owned me. Knowing I wouldn't ever get the chance to show her that truth wrecked what little sanity I clung to. Something had to fucking give, or I feared I was going to go off the deep end like my brother.

22

MILA

Marshal Pritt called with an update, but not the one I'd hoped to hear. The two Demons were still on the loose, but according to him, I had nothing to fear. Of course not. Tension rode my shoulders into absolute knots, and I barked at Devon more than usual.

"What's the problem, Mom," he finally confronted me, hands on hips while I sat at the table long after dinner rather than outside, my tea in my hands.

I heaved a sigh and confessed to what I'd known for almost two weeks. "Two of the Demons escaped house arrest."

"Fuck."

Not bothering to chide him, I nodded at the sentiment.

"What does Pritt say?" Devon asked.

"Not much," I muttered. "He says we're safe right where we are, that no one has ever gotten injured under their protection."

"There's always a first."

"Right?" I huffed another heavy breath and closed my eyes.

"So what are we gonna do?"

"Stay put." I looked up at him. "What else can we do? We have no stash of money, no connections. I don't even have a gun."

He chewed on the inside of his lip for a few seconds. "We could probably get one from Vigil."

"No," I snapped.

"What else is wrong, Mom?"

I couldn't help but smile sadly at my son's intuition.

"Does it have something to do with him?"

My smile faded. "You need to stay away from him. It's definitely for the best."

"If staying away from him is a good thing then why are you miserable?"

Devon had a point, and I nodded at the tea in my

mug before glancing up once more to read his face. "I wasn't kind to him."

My son shrugged like it was no big deal, but a wily twinkle lit his eyes. "Then make it up to him."

"Devon." I pursed my lips.

"Take him *cookies*, Mom. Sheesh, your mind is always in the gutter when it comes to Vigil."

I side-eyed him while he turned to rifle through the snack cabinet.

"Why don't you go over for a little visit," he said, pulling down a bag of pizza Combos. "Make things right so I can have my best friend back."

"I thought you had a new best friend."

"Yeah, but he'll never compare to Vigil." Devon popped a few Combos into his mouth and watched me.

No one could compare with Vigil, I feared, not just for Devon but myself as well—and the man hadn't even touched me in the way we definitely both craved. Could I make things right? Did I want to? Maybe for Devon, but for myself...

"No sex," I muttered out loud when I should have kept the thought inside.

"Don't see why you abstain. He likes and wants you. You want him."

I frowned up at my son. "You forgot the part about *me* liking *him*."

"Come on." He rolled his eyes and dug another handful of cheese stuffed pretzels from the bag. "There isn't anything about that man you don't like."

"I don't like that he's a biker."

"Don't you?" Devon eyed me, all trace of teasing gone from his dark eyes as he peered at me. "If he wasn't a club member, I doubt he'd be so protective. I doubt he'd be as loyal to his loved ones as he is."

I considered the situation Vigil had told me about with his brother and how the troubles had definitely affected him emotionally. He loved his brother, I had zero doubt. He also loved my son—again, no doubt. He'd also claimed out loud that I belonged to him. Did that mean he loved me, too?

Sagging in my chair, I attempted a smile.

"Just go talk to him," Devon said. "I'll lock the door behind you—but take your phone and keep it on you just in case you need me to come rescue you or something."

I laughed lightly. "Are you becoming the helicopter parent now?"

"Nah. I'm encouraging you to head out into the great unknown, take what you want, and enjoy the hell out of that fun."

"Devon Zeigler!"

He laughed and took off for the living room. "Just be *safe!*"

Little turd. But he had a point. Vigil loved hard outside of the bedroom and he didn't cut off his emotions. I'd seen traces of anger, but not the unusual sort that raised red flags. I did love his protective nature, how he didn't hide his thoughts and feelings from me. Vigil had zero filter on his mouth, but I'll admit to liking that, too.

So did I like him?

Yes, yes I do.

Did I want him?

I craved him. His nearness. Those hands, those damn hands that had gotten me off better than any man's cock...

Lips pursed, I considered the war inside my head and heart. There was no denying the connection between us, the electric charge of energy whenever he entered the room. So what to do?

"You're over-thinking this, Mom!" Devon hollered from the living room.

I thought for another minute before getting up from the table and dumping my tea down the drain.

Devon didn't breathe a word as I went back to the bathroom and showered. He didn't even look my way when I walked back through the living room dressed rather than bumbling around in my robe like I'd been doing every night for the past couple of days.

"Lock up, baby."

He shuffled out to the kitchen behind me and gave me a quick hug from behind, kissing the top of my head. "Be happy, Mom."

When had he gotten so damn tall? Tears pricked my eyelids, but I stepped outside without acknowledging the rare affection, waiting for the lock to click behind me.

I breathed in deeply until it hurt, filling my lungs with cooler night air. A few crickets or night time insects chipped along as I slipped across the yards, comforted more by the cell tucked in my back pocket so my son could reach me with a quick swipe and speed dial.

My heart thumped heavily in my chest, and my shoulders stayed damn tight against my ears.

Through the slider, I could see Vigil sitting in his living room, and I paused at bottom of the two stairs leading up to his back deck, my breath loud in my ears, my entire body shaking.

Had I wasted that long shower and shave? Had I ruined my chance of even having him as a friend by being such a bitch the week before? He'd stayed away as ordered while most asshole bikers would have just taken what they wanted.

Vigil was different. I knew that inside the deepest part of me.

And I did want him. Body, mind, heart ... soul. Every inch of me longed for him.

He turned his head as though he could feel my inner turmoil, and our gazes clashed, raising the hairs along my arms. Without taking his focus off me, he set his cell aside, rose to his feet, and walked to the slider.

My feet stayed rooted.

The sound of the door sliding open barely registered through the pulse thrumming in my ears.

"Mila?"

"Can I come in?" I whispered, my stomach twisting even as warmth swept over me at the sight of his bare chest and the gray sweats hanging low on his hips.

"Of course." He stepped back, and I forced my shaking legs to carry me up and across the deck. Slipping past him filled my nose with his clean scent, weakening my knees even more. "Come here, wildcat."

He moved in and crushed me to his chest in a

blink, and I melted. Fucking went liquid like a slab of butter in the August heat, puddling in both my heart and panties. He smelled divine, and the heat and hardness of his torso felt even better than I'd remembered.

"How did you know?" I muttered against his chest, drinking in his affection like a parched, panting cat.

"You looked like you needed a hug." His voice rumbled beneath my ear, and I sighed. "A little turd might have texted to tell me you were on your way over and to not let you hightail it back to your place without finding the nerve to talk to me first, too."

"Turd is right." I laughed and pulled back enough to look up into his face. "I'm sorry."

"For what?"

"Being a bitch."

"Mmm." A twinkle lay in his eyes. "I ought to spank your gorgeous ass red, but I don't hit women."

My smile faded at the sincerity in his eyes. He knew. Somehow, he fucking knew—and I'd never even told Devon of what all my ex had done to me behind closed doors. At least the asshole had made sure the bruises and marks he left on my skin could be covered by clothing.

"And how did you know he was abusive?"

"Your tells, wildcat. The things you've said, the way you flinched if I moved around you too quickly."

"I do?"

"Yeah."

"Well, shit. Guess I have some PTSD I wasn't aware of."

He smoothed back my hair, and my eyelids fluttered shut. "Will you let me spoil you tonight?"

I nuzzled my cheek in his rough palm as my nipples tightened. "What'd you have in mind?"

"Stripping you down," he said against my forehead, his soft lips and beard brushing over my skin. "Touching every inch of your body, massaging every muscle until you soften into my bed and refuse to leave."

"Massage, huh?"

"Just a massage—unless you need or want more, yeah."

Goddamn this man...

"Your eyes say yes, wildcat. What's your mouth going to say?"

"Massage for me, but then I get a chance to see what you've got going on inside those hot as fuck sweats."

"Deal," he tossed out before I even finished speaking.

Laughing, I accepted his outstretched hand, and he tugged me toward the stairs.

23

VIGIL

Sure, we had a shit ton of stuff to talk about. Make right, but Mila had come over, vulnerability plastered on her face, and I knew my waiting, my planning would finally come to fruition.

I'd gotten a text from Devon telling me exactly what I'd told her, but he also texted he didn't want to see her home before sunrise. Little punk. He'd never get an argument out of me, though. Having his blessing to pursue his mom meant more to me than I'd ever considered with a woman before. It eased a bit of that ache in my chest. Made that feeling of rightness in my gut solidify into a block of defined truth.

I'd told Mila she belonged to me, and I didn't doubt one goddamn syllable of that sentence.

Now I'm going to show her.

I led Mila upstairs to my room and kicked aside the damp towel I'd tossed to the floor once I hopped out of the shower. At least I'd put new sheets on the bed the day before. I ripped back my comforter.

"Strip and get comfortable belly-down, wildcat. Be back in a minute."

She stared after me, eyes wide.

"What?" I asked, pausing in the bathroom door.

"You're not going to watch? Tell me what piece of clothing to peel off first and all that shit?"

"Baby," I let her see the lust racing through me in my eyes, "if I stick around for that sort of lead up, I'll never get those muscles hitched up around your ears to relax. When it's time, I'll enjoy every goddamn inch of you, Mila. Don't your worry your pretty little head."

I turned and left her alone, taking my time getting the bottle of massage oil I'd purchased and put away for the day she gave into letting me touch her skin and working her muscles with the hands she lusted after. I grabbed a couple of towels and paused, giving her time to do as I'd told her to.

My feet itched to move, so I gave in and caught her on her knees, stretching out to lay on her belly.

Goddamn, that ass...

Forget talking down the chub. My fucking dick shot upward without its usual constraining jeans or leathers I usually wore in her presence. I tucked the swelling head back inside my sweat's band and gripped my girth while moving back into my room.

"Comfortable?" I asked, my voice gruff.

"Kind of."

"What's wrong, wildcat?"

"I just need you to touch me already," she whispered, turning her head to glance up at me, but her gaze snagged on my tented sweats. "Show me that a man's hands can be gentle."

Anger wanted to rise over thoughts of the abuse she'd lived through, but the flick of her tongue along her lower lip brought a groan to mine. I squeezed my girth again, fighting for restraint as she continued to stare at my groin.

"I want to feel you inside me—skin on skin."

Fuck. Me. "Birth control?"

She finally lifted her focus to my eyes off my throbbing dick. "I can't get pregnant."

Her tells said it all, the pain in her eyes, the fucking anger, but I refused to focus on thoughts of what her cocksucking ex had done to her to make her incapable of carrying another child.

"I'm clean, surprisingly," she continued as

though my hesitancy meant I needed talking into taking her bare.

I nodded. "Same. Now close your eyes, wildcat. Let me take care of you."

Smiling, she obeyed, and I uncapped the oil, drizzling the liquid in lazy streaks along her back. I set the bottle aside and glided my hands gently through the oil, coating every inch of her back to the swell of her ass.

A sweet sigh escaped her, the furrow between her brows disappearing.

Properly coated, I pressed harder, using my thumbs to rub along muscle and bone, no sound between us but our breathing and the occasional whispered moan from Mila as I worked her back. The tension in her shoulders took some time, but she eventually grew pliant and soft like I wanted.

But I wasn't anywhere near done learning every inch of her.

I drizzled oil down both legs, working those muscles at the same time, making my way slowly up over the globes of her ass, my stare on the darkness between. My dick fucking leaked like a mad man, smearing and straining inside my sweats.

Edging toward the end of my restraint, I gently pressed on the insides of her thighs, and she opened for me. The pink petals of her pussy glistened, moisture already dripped onto my sheets. A slick mess.

I swallowed the sudden rush of saliva and poured some oil in my palm. A turn of my wrist dribbled some down her ass crack, and I followed with my hand, the heat of her, the whimper and lift of her hips tightening my groin to the point of pain.

Teeth clenched, I rubbed over her again, my fingertips sliding alongside her swollen clit and back up.

"Vigil," she whispered as a plea, and I gave her what she wanted, sliding my middle finger deep inside her hot core. She groaned and lifted her hips, but I pressed against her spine with my other hand, holding her still, slowly working my finger in and out of her, drinking down her whimpers when I added a second.

I lowered my other hand on her spine to its base, my thumb rubbing over her puckered hole. She didn't tense with the touch, and the husky groan she let out when I pressed my tip into her told me what I'd been dying to know.

She wasn't adverse to me taking her there.

I popped the top of my dick free from my sweats and swept my thumb over the soaked tip. Pre-cum smeared over my thumb—and I rubbed it all over her asshole, my dick jerking at the thought of claiming her there.

Soon.

Her ass sucked my thumb and pre-cum in deeper, and I began fucking both her holes in opposition, slick, slow glides in and out until she panted and whimpered on every exhale, her hips moving in time with me.

"Going to come," she moaned.

I growled my encouragement, and her breath caught, her body tightening. "Cream all over my hand, Mila."

Without a touch to her clit, she shuddered and cried out my name, hands grasping at my sheets above her head, her lower body grinding against my hands. Her pussy convulsed around my fingers, the ooze of wetness my own goddamn breaking point.

She hadn't completely come down, but I couldn't wait any longer.

I shoved off my sweats, my balls seized tight against my body, and climbed between her thighs. A quick lift beneath her hips set her on her knees, but I pressed slowly into her pussy, the tight clamp around my head gritting my teeth.

Soaked. Slick. Fucking hot and tight as hell...

Her pussy took me inch by inch, her back arching, and body trembling as I fought to remain in control. Gentle.

"Vigil..."

I pulled out to the head and worked my way back in, her sweet pussy stretching to take me all the way until my balls rested against her. "Goddamn, wildcat," I groaned through my teeth.

Buried to the hilt in fucking heaven ... but I needed her closer.

I wound my arm beneath her and sat back, pulling her up onto her knees, holding her tight against my chest. "You're fucking perfect, Mila." I eased out of her and pushed back in, grasping her chin to turn her face toward me.

Her lips parted, her eyes clenched shut, and her brow furrowed as I forced myself to go slow, dragging out and thrusting back in against her cervix.

"You've got every inch of my dick buried inside you, wildcat. Feel me?"

"God yes," she groaned.

I thrust a bit harder, pulling a gasp from her lips, one of pure fucking lust, not fear or pain.

"This pussy is mine." I slid my hand down over her soft belly, sliding my fingers alongside my dick as I pumped in and out of her. Gathering her cream,

I slid them back up to her hard nub and rubbed along either side.

"Yes," she moaned as her pussy clenched down on me. "More, Vigil. Please."

I snapped.

I took her mouth, her hands reaching back to grasp at my hair, and I bucked into her, my fingers rubbing her clit.

She arched and moaned, her tongue lashing at mine, her body writhing in my tight hold. Plundering took on a whole new meaning for me as my dick took control—I fucking gave into the lust for her, the need to claim her fully, every hard thrust of my hips pulling a pleading whimper for more from her.

"I want your come on my dick," I growled against her mouth, shoving against her womb. "Come with me, wildcat." I pressed harder on her clit and rubbed, and she gave me what I wanted. "Fuck, yeah."

She arched, her pussy clamping down on my dick to the point I saw fucking stars.

"That's it, baby." I thrust again—wetness coated me. Buried deep as my balls tingled. The first shot of cum through my dick tightened my entire body rigid, and I groaned into Mila's neck, the rush of euphoria like none I'd known. My spunk filled her the fuck up. Dribbled out around my plunging dick as I continued to fuck in and out of her, draining every last drop I had to give.

She shuddered and sagged against me, and I finally stilled, holding her close, sniffing and licking along her neck, filling my lungs with her sweetness.

"Okay, wildcat?"

"Mmm." She tilted her head to the side and covered my hand still on her pussy with her own, her fingers feeling where I still stretched her. Her gentle rubbing, her moving my hand against her— the slight gyration of her hips went straight to my fucking head.

"Lay down, baby." I eased her toward the bed.

"Don't stop."

"Not gonna." I nipped her shoulder as she sprawled on my mattress, my dick still buried in her pussy.

Planking, I watched my semi glide in and out of the mess we'd made, every slow drag out of heaven making me want more. So much more.

I sat back on my haunches and spread her cheeks wide, giving me a better view. Her pink petals stretched around me, but I wanted her ass.

She welcomed my thumb, her hips rising as a

low moan escaped her. "You gonna let me have this, too?" I asked, my voice rasped to hell as her oil-coated asshole let my thumb sink in deep.

"Whatever you want, Vigil—it's yours," she said through the dark hairs lying across her face. Eyes closed, her face relaxed, I slid my thumb back out and slowly pressed back in.

My dick jerked in her pussy.

"Hold on, wildcat." I pulled out, caught the ooze of cum leaking from her hole and smeared it up over her ass. "We're going to have some fun."

y ass wasn't a virgin, but at the press of his cock against my hole, I caught my breath and lip between my teeth. He'd felt huge inside my pussy, filling me beyond what I'd thought possible, but my ass...

Fuck, it burned. Tears squeezed out of my clenched eyelids as he pressed in. I fought to stay relaxed, told myself to push back, but holy hell.

"Mila?"

"Don't stop."

He pressed harder.

"Too big," I heard myself gasp as his head finally slid past my ring wishing to keep him out. "Holy fuck, too big."

"Shh." He leaned over my back, his chest like a furnace to my already heated skin. "Worst is over."

Like hell, it was. Vigil was a man of restraint—no doubt about that, but I knew a beast lived inside his soul. He'd yet to unleash it, but he would. If I gave him permission.

He ran his hands up and down my back, giving me time to adjust.

"More," I whispered the second I thought I couldn't handle it.

One flex of his ass gained him another inch, and I winced, grasping at his sheets again, whimpering.

"I got you, wildcat." He licked the shell of my ear, nibbled on my jaw, keeping the full weight of him on his elbows beside me. A slight pull out and another press stretched me, the raw burn curling my toes— and setting off sparks throughout my entire body.

"Oh God," I whispered, trying to lift toward him when he repeated the action.

"Fuck," he groaned against my ear, his beard tickling, his cock fucking *killing* me.

"Vigil." I gasped as he pressed in deeper. Holy fuck, deeper...

"Goddamn, wildcat." He gulped and planked, leaving my back cold. "Your ass is so goddamn tight." The stinging drag out—the gentle thrust back in—

he growled like a damn animal as he finally bottomed out. "Fuck."

Vigil rested his forehead on my back and stilled deep inside me. "Fuck." He trembled, and I forced myself to relax.

"Take me," I whispered, opening my eyes and turning my head enough to see him shaking. "Don't hold back. Please."

"Hurt you."

"You won't. I want it, Vigil. I know it's you—I'm not afraid."

He growled like an animal—and gave into that beast.

I bit back my shriek as he pulled out and plowed into me like a damn train, sliding me along the sheets.

Holy fuck ... holy fuck.

So deep. Brutally so. Every thrust harder than the one before, every grunt and groan from his mouth oozing wetness from my pussy. I buried my face in his bed and shrieked, "Yes!" with every thrust, my muffled cries only seeming to spur him on.

He sank back onto his knees and lifted my hips, creating a deep arch in my back.

I needed to come. Needed release—hell, I

needed him to find his so he would stop even as I craved more.

He palmed my pussy before I moved my hand to take care of business myself. "This pussy is mine."

"Yes," I gasped as he pinched my clit.

"This ass is mine."

I saw stars behind my eyelids as he slammed in deep. "Fuck, yes."

My climax hit me like a tsunami, and I shrieked, bucking in his hold. I couldn't help the rush of wetness squirting from my body, coating his hand. Soaking his bed.

"God*damn*, Mila." Vigil let loose, his bruising grip on my hips holding me still as he fucked me hard and deep, the curses groaning past his lips, the grunts ripping from his chest keeping me on a steady high. My pulse thrummed and ears rang as I lay pliant in his hold, allowing him to use me for his own pleasure.

He'd given me so much already...

Wet heat shot deep inside me, and his animalistic groan shivered over me, pebbling my skin. A few more thrusts, and the pain of him inside me eased. We both heaved for breath, and he sank with me into the mattress, his sweaty chest against me, his lips searching through my hair for the skin of my neck.

A shudder rippled through him as he licked the dampness from my skin.

I turned my face on a harsher angle, needing his mouth. He gave me what I needed, the soft cushion of his lips, the gentle glide of his tongue along mine curling my toes in exquisite perfection.

Unable to move beneath him, I soaked in his heat, his hardness, the feeling of absolute rightness.

Eventually, he released my mouth and brushed his lips over my ear. "Don't move."

"Deal," I whispered with a smile, but he backed out of my ass and a wince flatlined my lips.

"Did I hurt you?"

"You're a goddamn beast, Vigil—but I loved it."

He chuckled and kissed the base of my spine.

Every muscle in my body felt depleted like Jell-O. Relaxed to the point of passing out. I obeyed, not moving as Vigil returned to the bed with a warm, wet towel, gently wiping between my thighs.

"I ought to take you into the shower, but I can barely move," he said, running a hand up over my back.

I patted the mattress beside me, and he stretched

out, pulling me into his arms, away from the wetness I'd made on his bed.

Chest to chest. Legs entwined. He kissed my forehead, my nose, and finally my lips with gentle brushes and flicks of his tongue, tasting and sharing my breath.

"Sorry about the mess," I whispered.

"It was hot as fuck."

My damn smile came easy.

"Gonna make you a deal, wildcat." He pulled back, and my heart stuttered at the emotion in his pale, sleepy eyes. So vulnerable and open, completely unshuttered, allowing me in. "You're going to unload everything you've been going through the last year, and I'm going to listen without getting pissed. I'll take and carry that burden and promise not to kill anyone in return."

I couldn't help the laughter bubbling inside me. "I'd rather hear your dark secrets."

A flicker of something slid over his face—fear perhaps? "Tonight is yours, wildcat. Get all the shit out then let me hold you while you sleep."

"I have to go home, Vigil—I can't leave Devon there alone."

"He told me he'd castrate me if you got home before sunrise."

I slapped at his shoulder, and he chuckled. "My son did not say that."

"Not those exact words, but I know a threat when a man makes one."

"Man, huh?" I cocked an eyebrow, loving the teasing light in Vigil's eyes.

"He's seen more than most kids his age."

My smile faded. "He has."

"Tell me."

So, I did. From the verbal and emotional abuse my son had endured, to the physical assaults I'd dealt with in private. It'd been the final beating, the one that ruined my womb for life that had broken the camel's back.

But it was time to move on.

25

VIGIL

Mila didn't hold a goddamn thing back, and guilt over wanting to do the opposite with her sat heavy on my head long after she fell asleep wrapped around my body. My heart ached for her, the devastation she'd endured, the secrets of abuse she'd hid from her son. Fuck, he knew enough as it was.

I smoothed my hand down her back, her skin like satin against my fingertips.

Sleep eluded me even though my clock glared an angry red two a.m. from the bed stand. I'd never exhausted myself with a woman before, but Mila had drained me dry—of cum and emotions, including the ones over Ricky. I'd been buried in pussy and ass before, but never felt beyond the flesh.

The connection between me and Mila ... I felt that clear to the tips of my fucking toes. Didn't doubt the claiming I'd laid on her, and the fact she'd whispered and groaned her agreement, I knew I was set for life.

Mila was mine. So was her son.

I'd texted Devon one-handed not long after his mom fell asleep with her head on my chest letting him know she wouldn't be home until morning. He replied with two thumbs up emojis and a "Good!" making me grin.

I rolled both of us, spooning against her back, one arm around her waist and holding her lush ass against my groin. My dick chubbed, but I talked the fucker down. I wanted her again, but I wasn't an asshole. I'd wait until she woke on her own.

She sighed in her sleep, and I made myself close my eyes to shut out the dark. Mila belonged in my bed, with me every goddamn night, and since she'd agreed to my claiming, I wasn't about to let her go back on it.

Fuck Stacy Pritt and fuck the widow's son and his rental.

Mila and Devon would be moving in with me before the weekend ended. I couldn't stand the thought of them *not*. Wouldn't stand for it at all.

I'd lost Ricky, but I wasn't about to lose the two new loves I'd found.

I breathed in Mila's sweet scent, laid my hand over her heart, and counted the steady beats until finally passing the fuck out.

26

MILA

I woke at the crack of dawn as usual, but snuggly warm and completely relaxed. A few blinks brought the unfamiliar room into focus—and the night before rushed back to mind. My pulse lit as I realized that snuggly warmth was actually a hard body pressed against my back from neck to toes.

Vigil's steady, warm breaths stirred the hairs at my nape, one of his legs thrust between mine, my toes resting on his shin. He still slept, I realized as his exhales remained even.

I took a few minutes to enjoy waking in his arms and how his heat radiated through every inch of my body to the point of tingling in all the best places. A shuddering sigh ripped through me while I grinned like an idiot. I'd had *fun* alright. Even though he'd been gentle until the end, sex with Vigil had been toe curling, oxygen stealing, and ass achingly perfection.

I considered turning and waking him with my hand and mouth since I hadn't gotten the chance to the night before, but thoughts of my son waking to find me still gone decided for me.

Easing from Vigil's heavy limbs without waking him was like playing pick-up sticks, but I won. I couldn't decide if I was pleased by that fact or not.

Cool air slid over my naked body as I studied him sprawled across his king-sized bed. That sheet we'd had atop us pulled down to his hip, but didn't reveal the goods beneath. Lower lip between my teeth, I gently inched it downward with one hand and nearly let out a moan at the sight of him. Morning wood hadn't yet crept up on him, but he still hung thick and long over his thigh. How the hell had that monster fit inside me?

Wetness rose between my legs at the memory of his slow thrusts in and out of me, and my sore ass clenched at the thought of his beast coming out to play.

Good god almighty.

I grabbed my cell and clothes off the chair in the corner where I'd left them the night before and slipped out of his bedroom into the hallway. A quick change in the downstairs bathroom, and I hurried home, the tweeting of birds and the rising sun on my face a sign of a new beginning beyond what I'd ever dreamed.

My face heated as I considered what Devon would say but told myself being open and honest with him would lead the way for him to be the same when the time came.

At least, I hoped.

I fished the back door's key from its hiding place beneath the stoop and let myself in. Silence met my ears, but I hadn't expected Devon to be up yet. He'd left his bedroom door cracked open like he'd always requested since a toddler, so I stood and watched him sleep for a few minutes, my heart overflowing to the point tears stung my eyes.

Smiling, and my footsteps light, I returned to the kitchen and made coffee, sitting my sore butt at the table with a mug and buttered toast to wait for him.

My cell dinged, and thinking it was Vigil, heat rushed over my skin. Grinning, I grabbed it up and swiped across the screen.

Marshal Pritt: **Your husband escaped while in transit this morning**

I blinked, read the line again, my chest tight and breath held.

No.

Why the hell would he text such information? I rang him, my heart pounding.

"Hey."

Hey? All nonchalant and sleepy? "What the fuck, Pritt?" I managed to make my vocal cords work.

"Calm down, Michelle. We've got this under control."

"Calm down?" I squeaked, my throat swelling with rage. "The last thing he said while being dragged away was that he would get revenge. Burn both me and my son to the ground. Tell me again why I should calm down?"

"He has no clue where you are. None whatsoever, and—"

"How the fuck do you know that?" My voice found strength, rising with the anger coursing through me.

Pritt let out a heavy exhale like he was annoyed, the bastard. "There are only a handful of people in the agency who know where you are."

"And he's got contacts out the ass, Pritt. Now that he's out, he'll want to find us, and he will."

Devon rounded the corner, shirtless and hair mussed, his brow furrowed. "Mom?"

"I can come over later this afternoon," Pritt continued, his voice still unmoved and bored as could be, "but honestly, I don't think we need to over react,"

Over react. If Stacy Pritt had a child of his own looking at him like Devon did at me in that moment, my tells showing on my face for my baby to see, he wouldn't be so quick to say such a thing.

I needed a gun.

I needed to pack up our shit and leave.

Immediately.

"I'll call you later," I said and hung up without waiting for a reply. "He escaped."

"Fuck." Devon's face paled, and I hopped up, throwing my arms around him. He actually clung to me, and I closed my eyes, wishing to hold his head to my chest like I'd done when he'd been little.

"We're going to be okay," I whispered, fighting off tears. "I'm not going to sit around here waiting for the marshal—I'll figure something out."

"Call Vigil." Devon stepped out of my hold and grasped my arms. "Call him. Now. He'll protect us." His dark eyes peered intently at me as I nibbled on my inner lip.

Yes, Vigil would offer us his protection, but I couldn't bear the thought of bringing danger to his doorstep. "I can't put him in that position," I whispered, my heart aching as much as my throat.

Devon's scowl deepened. "The man is madly in love with you and isn't going to just let you take off, Mom. We're stuck with him whether you want it or not—especially since you spent the night in his bed."

My face heated. "He's not in love with me."

"Bullshit."

"Dev..." I raised an eyebrow, but he didn't show one ounce of being contrite over the curse.

"Calling it like it is, and I won't apologize."

We had a stare down, our first one in a long, long time. Usually, he caved to my authority, but I recognized the stubborn tilt of his jaw, the set of his shoulders hitching toward his ears.

A slow smile tilted the corners of my lips. "Love you, Dev."

"Love you more," he said, his dimple popping within a flash. "Now call your man so I don't have to freak over not being strong enough to protect you myself."

Those damn tears hazed my vision again, and I nodded. "Okay."

27

VIGIL

My cell dinged, and I peeled an eyelid up. Mila wasn't beside me.

I sat up abruptly, my head jerking toward the bathroom. The door hung open, the lights off.

"Mila?" I hollered while grabbing my cell.

Wildcat: **He escaped.**

"Goddamnit all to fucking hell." I scrubbed a hand down over my face, knowing exactly what she'd meant. I put through a call rather than text a reply.

"Vigil."

"You okay?" I asked, climbing out of bed and grabbing my jeans off the floor.

"Yeah." Her voice shook—a nice, little lie.

"What'd that fucker Pritt say?"

"Says we have nothing to worry about."

"Bullshit." I yanked up my jeans and strode into the bathroom to take care of business, not giving a shit I was on the phone. "I can protect you in ways the agency can't. Do you trust me?"

"Yes."

A rush of relief swept over me even though my entire body tensed tight as fuck. "Pack your bags, Mila, enough for at least a week, but don't worry about food. I'll be over in five to pick you up."

"Okay." She hung up, no questions asked, and my chest ached like a motherfucker.

She did trust me. Explicitly.

I grabbed a bag from my closet and rang Warden.

"What's up?" he asked, his voice muffled.

I glanced at the clock—it read only six-seventeen. "Long fucking story, but I've got to take off north with my woman and her kid."

"Claimed her, huh?"

"Shut the fuck up," I growled at his teasing tone. "They're both mine, and I'll protect them no matter the cost."

"I understand," he stated, all business.

"Can we go to Shaun's camp?"

"Of course." His voice came through clearer like he'd sat up, fully awake. "What's going on?"

"Mila's ex is Harlon Flanders, and he's loose and gunning for her."

"Who's Mila?"

"Michelle." Exasperation swept through me, and I slammed my shirt drawer closed hard enough the entire chest of drawers shook. "I'm going to have you, Ryker, and Devil stay here to look after the club."

"Wait. Michelle's ex is *Harlon Flanders*?"

"You fucking heard me."

"The fuck? And you said he escaped?"

"Don't know how the fuck he managed, but yeah. I'm taking all of your employees if I can. The Thompson twins, too."

"That's fine—whatever you need, we've got your back, Vig."

"I've got a few more calls to make, but I need you to call Ryker and fill him in for me." I hung up without a goodbye and rang Devil, needing to be caught up on the security we had set in place at the acreage in Maine. While there wasn't a chain link fence around the property like we had at the club, it was far enough away to protect the other patched members and their old ladies if shit went down.

Of course Devil had the entire camp set up with security cameras from every angle except inside the cabins. I put him on full-time watch dog, telling him to grab another brother as backup.

I called Stone next, Warden's top sentry for his security firm, and he agreed to come along, leaving Giada at home.

Bag in hand, I thumped down the stairs in my unlaced boots. "Call Greed, Sin, Hammer, and Crow," I told Stone. "Tell them to get their asses to the club, too."

"They coming along with us?"

"Yep. Warden, Ryker, and Devil have the club."

"Gotcha. I'll bring my gear. Food?" Always the level-headed, prepared one, Stone.

"We'll meet up at the club and grab shit on the way. I want to be out of town by seven, latest."

"You got it."

Shoving my cell in my back pocket, I let out a few curses. I'd found fucking heaven, and shit had to go down. I *knew* it'd been too damn quiet.

I didn't doubt Flanders' connections. As the Sergeant at Arms of the Demented Demons MC, the fucker had gotten away with taking out two of the Vegas Vipers eight or so years earlier in a shootout. The clubs had always been combative, but that loss of life had cemented a rivalry that'd only calmed in the couple of years prior to their being taken down by the FBI.

"Fucking cocksuckers." I tossed my bag in the back of my truck and pulled out of the driveway, ripping around the corner, and slamming it back into park in Mila's driveway a few seconds later.

Devon yanked open the door as I stalked up the front walkway. Fear had his face pale and eyes wide, and I pulled him in for a quick squeeze the second I got through the doorway. "You okay, Dill?"

"Yeah."

"Got your shit packed?"

"Yes, sir."

I clasped his shoulder and moved back towards the hallway, hearing Mila scrambling in her bedroom. She pulled clothes from her bottom drawer, but I didn't take the time to admire her fine backside. As though she felt my presence, she jerked upright and spun. Hair and eyes wild, her shoulders slumped and she let out a half-sob as her gaze landed on me.

Two steps took me into her personal space, and I pulled her up into my arms, burying my face in her hair. "Gonna be okay, wildcat. I got you."

She sniffed, her body trembling, and I know she

fought for calm to keep from freaking Devon out even more.

"Where we going?" Devon asked from behind me.

"Warden's old lady has a camp up in Maine. We're meeting a couple of brothers at the club and taking off from there. The place is tight with security, and it's not a place too many people know about. We'll be safe there."

Devon let out a heavy exhale. "What do you need me to do, Vigil?"

"Just get your shit and your ass in my truck."

"Okay."

I leaned back from Mila, holding her face in my palms. Wetness coated her eyes, making them glow a golden brown, and I swiped the tear tracks from her cheeks with my thumbs. "I won't let him anywhere near Devon."

She nodded, a trembling smile lifting her lips the slightest bit. "I know."

I kissed her forehead, allowing myself a moment to linger, breathing in her sweetness. "Let's go, wildcat."

28

MILA

I sat curled in Vigil's front seat, arms wrapped around my upturned legs. Silence filled the cab, but a non-stop thumping sounded in my ears. I couldn't calm my racing heart. The only time I'd been able to breathe had been when Vigil wrapped his arms around me in my bedroom and I cried. That feeling of safety hadn't ever been so real, and I realized that I did trust him, fully.

Vigil hadn't once taken advantage of me or Devon, and he was willing to put his life, his brothers' lives in danger in order to protect us.

My throat tightened again as I considered my son on the seat behind me, and the two trucks following on our tail. We'd been at the Vipers club for less than ten minutes waiting for the others who he'd asked to come along with us.

Stone, Greed, and Sin were all in the security business, employees for Warden, Vigil's enforcer. Hammer and Crow were two blond giants, construction workers with shoulders and breadth to rival Vigil. Coldness lay in all five sets of eyes, unsmiling lips and stern countenances enough to make any person quake.

Devon drank it in, even smiling, the little turd.

I didn't want the MC lifestyle for him, and gave him stern looks of my own while trying to pal it up with the bikers.

Ricky hadn't been around, or at least that I could tell—Vigil didn't introduce us to anyone beyond the five coming along north with us. We shot up Route 95 a few minutes before seven, Hammer and his twin brother Crow stopping over the New Hampshire border to grab a "shit ton" of groceries at Vigil's order.

While I still worried at my fingernails, chewing them to the quick, I knew the ways of an MC when someone fell under their protection. I also knew what it meant when a patched member claimed a woman.

I was good and truly fucked, my life no longer

my own, and while fear clawed at my gut that I might be making a mistake, I took comfort in the fact I knew without a shadow of a doubt that Devon would be safe. Safer than any marshal of the Witness Protection Agency could keep him.

No law constrained Vigil and his club. No letter that needed to be followed. They would punch, stab, or shoot first and ask questions later, leaving little chance for danger to befall us.

I heaved a heavy sigh and tipped my head back, closing my eyes even as guilt over putting them all at risk churned my stomach.

Vigil entwined his fingers through mine, and I put my feet on the floor, clasping his hand in both mine atop my lap.

"Thank you," I whispered without opening my eyes.

"Anything for you," he whispered back and squeezed my fingers.

Flutters drowned out the worry eating at my mind for a brief moment, and I turned my head against the rest to look at him. He stared straight ahead, face set, a slight furrow still denting his brow. Leaning forward slightly, Vigil seemed to think he could get into Maine before his truck would.

I bit back my smirk and turned to find Devon

staring out the smaller window behind Vigil. Such a trooper, that kid. He'd been to hell and back a few times over, and I wanted nothing more than a quiet, normal life for him.

Maybe someday we could have that.

My focus slipped to Vigil again, and I soaked in the strength of him, as though our clasped hands was all I needed to find comfort.

"What's the camp like?" Devon asked.

Vigil glanced out the rearview mirror before answering. "A couple of bunk houses. One main one for eating and shit. Over a hundred acres of woods out in the middle of nowhere, tucked up against a big lake."

"Will we all stay together?"

"There's two bedrooms in the main house—it's mostly an open concept living and dining area for the entire club," Vigil said. "We'll stay there, and the others will take the bunk houses on either side."

"I'll stay with the guys," Devon said.

"No you won't," I stated with finality. "You're sticking close to me. I don't want you out of my sight."

Devon frowned at me, but not out of anger, and I could feel Vigil's stare on my face.

"What?" I asked, angling to face Vigil, my tone pissy.

He turned his attention back on the road. "I understand you're scared and uptight, but you need to try to relax a little."

"It's called helicopter mom syndrome," Devon muttered from the backseat, and I shot him a glare. "What? You're damn good at it."

"Devon," I said, my tone stern, "this isn't a go out and ride your bike through the neighborhood kind of thing."

"Just trying to give you some space, Mom. Sheesh."

"I don't need space," I snapped, my stomach churning. "What I need is for you to just listen and not question orders!"

"That sounds familiar," he muttered, crossing his arms and staring out the window again.

I snapped my mouth shut at the retort that rose as his words lit to truthful light inside my head.

"Treat him as a sensitive being rather than one without feelings," Vigil said, his voice low, and I swallowed against the damn tightness in my throat —again.

Vigil had barked more than a dozen orders while

at the club, and his brothers had burst into action without a single complaint. No threats, no raised voices, or back talk, and they didn't do so out of fear like I'd spent the previous ten years watching—and experiencing.

His brothers respected his leadership. They weren't just loyal, but family in a way Harlon's club hadn't been.

There was no need for verbal or physical abuse when respect reigned.

"Sorry, Dev," I whispered past the lump in my throat. "Vigil's right—and so are you. You have every right to feelings and desires outside what I want for you. Just know I have your best interest at heart."

"I know, Mom." He offered a crooked smile that let me know he forgave me for acting like my ex.

I sat back in my seat, facing forward, and Vigil squeezed my fingers.

We settled into the house's main bedroom while Devon shacked up with Stone, Greed, and Sin. The twins showed up about an hour later with enough groceries to feed a damn army, and I set to putting everything away in the huge kitchen to keep my hands occupied.

Hammer slapped some burgers on an outside grill, and I managed to force one down along with some store-bought red bliss potato salad.

Stacy Pritt never tried calling me when I didn't reach out to him like I said I would. Not that I truly cared, but I decided to send a text letting him know we'd gone to a private camp in Maine for a while.

His simple, "OK" texted reply sent Vigil on a muttering rant about the asshole he'd gone to school with, the one who'd bullied him when they'd been kids. Devon eyed Vigil—then me—and I wondered as he quickly glanced away if my son knew something I didn't.

We sat by a campfire when the sun went down, and I indulged in a s'more while Devon packed away three, the scent of the fire's smoke and crackling embers soothing me enough to sit back in my chair. Although tension still clung to me and Vigil, the others were able to kick back entirely, joking with my son and treating him like one of their own.

I appreciated the curbing of swear words, but emotional exhaustion would have kept me from caring regardless.

"Tired?" Vigil murmured against the top of my hair.

I sat beside him in a folding chair, leaning against his shoulder, a heavy sweatshirt keeping the cool air off my back. "Yeah, a little."

"We can head into bed if you want."

The thought of a soft bed and Vigil's naked body sparked life between my thighs. I hadn't gotten a chance to take him in hand the night before, and the idea of doing so perked me up more than expected, all things considered. "Sounds good," I said, hoping the husk in my voice sounded more like tiredness than horny siren.

He took my hand and stood, pulling me along with him. "Dill's in your care, Stone."

Stone peered at me from across the fire, rather than Vigil. "I'll take care of him, Mila."

I found myself smiling, trusting yet another man I hardly knew. "I know."

"Won't let these two corrupt him, either," he said, backhanding Greed's chest and nodding his head at Sin on his other side. Both men swore under their breath, backhanding his shoulders at the same time, but all three chuckled rather than get into a full-on smack down like Demons would have done.

"I appreciate it." I turned toward my son, wishing

for a hug and kiss, but nodded when he winked at me. "Sleep tight, baby."

He tossed me a mock salute like I'd seen Vigil do a few times, and actually laughing lightly, I turned to follow Vigil into the dark, every step closer to privacy kicking up my pulse.

29

VIGIL

I had every intention of stripping down and just holding Mila, but the second she crawled beneath the blankets to join me, she disappeared beneath, her hands and mouth attacking my chubbed dick.

"Goddamn, wildcat." I clenched my jaw, tipped my head back, and tangled my fists in her hair.

She murmured her appreciation over my swelling dick between her lips, and I fought to keep from bucking upward, letting her explore and see what I was packing just like she'd wanted to do the night before.

"Thought you were tired," I said through gritted teeth as hers scraped up over my length with the perfect amount of bite. She had fucking teeth, alright. Thank *fuck*.

"Mmm." She popped off me and tossed back the covers, her dark hair a wild mess, her pupils eating at the chestnut ring around them. "My emotions have had it, but I only got a taste of you last night—not nearly enough."

I groaned a curse as she wrapped her lips around me again, taking me deep to the point I hit the back of her throat. Her hands took over below, slowly jacking me while she lathed with her tongue, swirling up over the head and back down.

"Fuck." I couldn't tear my gaze off her curtain of hair, her hollowed out cheeks—and when she lifted her gaze, I damn near came. Lust. Fucking adoration. Satisfaction. Fuck, I'd never seen a woman look so goddamn sexy while sucking my dick.

Unable to help myself, I nudged upward when she sank down my length, gagging her. I held her head still and did it again, growling like the fucking beast inside me wanting loose. Wasn't about to abuse her mouth like I'd done her ass the night before, though.

On the verge of blowing my load, I yanked her up over my body. "Fuck me," I ordered and claimed her mouth.

She shifted and did as told, slowly pressing back onto my dick, stuffing herself full to the goddamn hilt after a few shifts of her hips. A shudder rippled through her, and she moaned into my mouth. Holding still fucking hurt, but I tensed like a goddamn wooden board, unmoving except for my hands in her hair and my mouth on hers.

My fucking wildcat rode me like a sweet little pussy cat for all of thirty seconds before the claws came out. She scratched me with the fingernails she'd chewed ragged, her teeth snagging hold of my lower lip and pulling while she ground against my pelvis.

Fuck, yes.

I couldn't fucking breathe without smelling her—tasting her. Mila overloaded every sense, taking ownership of every inch of me, my heart and fucking head included.

Her breath hitched against my lips, and she let out a husky moan, her pussy clamping down around me.

I flipped us over and pounded into her, chasing the tingles brewing in my balls. Every grunt buried me deeper, every clutch of her heels at my ass pulled me tighter. Face buried in her neck, I bound my arms around her like a vise and gave her everything.

Every inch. Every heartbeat I had—I wanted her to have it all.

"Vigil," she groaned, and came again, creaming all over my dick and dripping off my balls.

I fucking exploded, trying to bury deeper, flexing my ass to tunnel straight through to her heart.

She clutched at me long after my dick stopped spurting against her womb, and I lazily rand my tongue along her lips, tasting the saltiness of her jawline and neck.

"I need a shower," she muttered, and I pulled out, but didn't let her go, snuggling her ass against my groin.

"No."

She laughed lightly and pinched my arm wound tight around her, but I wasn't having it.

"Stay here."

"I'm a sticky, cum-filled mess."

"Good." I nuzzled my face in her hair. "I like knowing my cum is inside you."

She huffed a sigh, but didn't move, and I grinned.

"I can't have kids," she stated quietly.

"Did you want more?"

"No," she didn't hesitate to reply.

"I never wanted one of my own, anyway." We lay

quietly for a time, and my nosiness got the best of me. "Is it his fault?"

She nodded, and I cursed internally, rolling her to face me. No tears laced her eyes, but pain enough lingered to send that damn ache across my chest.

"I'll never hurt you."

Her soft smile and the way she cupped my cheek had me wanting to nuzzle against her like her touch alone could sustain me. "I know, but I expect I might shy away without meaning too if you move too quickly around me."

I kissed her lips softly, that ache spreading, and I realized what it was—love. Didn't fucking doubt it, but wasn't about to toss that shit into the air and give Mila something else to concern herself with.

Nope. I'd just show the wildcat how I felt about her. She'd come around to accepting eventually, because no way in hell was I letting her go.

For two days, we fished in Moose Head Lake, sat around the campfire, and shot the shit. We ate pretty fucking good, too, since Hammer and Crow hadn't skimped, and Mila knew how to cook. I had that king of the castle feeling every damn night when she called us all to the table and set out a spread to feast upon.

Goddamn, what a woman. While I expected Greed the womanizer to ooze on the charm, even Sin, the quietest of my brothers, tossed out over a dozen compliments.

Guess she made an impact in my life because Stone and the others ribbed me for smiling more than usual—even considering our predicament and my missing brother. Couldn't fucking help it, though. Mila and Devon made me happy as shit. Guess I'd compartmentalized the shit in my head over Ricky in some way since his absence didn't hurt as much as it had in the beginning.

I hoped the best for him wherever he'd gone off to, and trusted fate to see him back home someday.

The third night, I lay sated by the love of my goddamn life, and my cell rang—Stone's ringtone I'd set for emergency only since he kept an eye on the cameras along with Devil.

I grabbed my phone off the bed stand, all trace of languid bliss shot to shit. "What's up?"

"Got two trucks just pulled in the driveway and are creeping up the lane—not ours."

"Fuck." I jumped out of bed, knowing we had all of three minutes before whoever approached on the winding, dirt road to the heart of the property pulled up out front. "Send Devon over here now and get everyone else in position. Call Ryker and get shit rolling."

We'd set plans in place in the event the security cameras at the property's entrance picked up anyone interested in knocking. Stone and my brothers knew what to do—and so did I, even though it was going to hurt like hell.

"Vigil?" Mila whispered, sitting with the blankets pulled up to her chest.

"We got company. Three minutes. Get dressed."

She hopped up like I'd lit a fire under her ass, her face pale and lips in a grim line.

I yanked on my clothes I'd torn off less than an hour earlier and shoved my feet into my boots. In the event shit went down, I'd set out a black sweatshirt and had my guns and other necessities atop the chest of drawers.

"Mom?" Devon called from down the hallway.

"Get to the bathroom," I barked, turning to find Mila dressed and holding out a hand.

"Give me a gun." Her face set in stone although her eyes betrayed her fear.

"Know how to use one?"

"Yes."

I handed over a Glock, and the sound of her checking the hammer steadied my pulse a bit. Fucking wildcat ... could she be any hotter?

The other Glock shoved in my waist band, a rifle slung over my shoulder, and nighttime goggles strapped to my head, compliments of Stone.

I led her into the bathroom and yanked open the closet door. At the back wall beneath the last shelf lay a hidden door. I dropped to my knees, pulled out the small laundry basket in front of it, and unhooked the hidden latch.

"Cool," Devon murmured as I backed away and stood.

"Gotta crawl through, but it opens up beyond the opening. There's flashlights hanging on the wall to the right and a set of stairs leading to a hidden basement."

"How long should we stay if things go bad?" Mila asked, her voice steady as Devon dropped and started crawling.

"I'd stay in the basement as long as you can. There's bottled water and some food, enough for three days at least, but don't come out this way. There's another door leading out of the basement—takes you out deep into the woods, a good hundred yards away from the house." I pulled her against me with a quick, hard hug, squeezing my eyes shut and giving myself three seconds of heaven—just in case. "You've got Ryker's number."

"Yeah."

"If I'm not back here to get you in a few hours, call him. He'll be on his way already, the rest of the Vipers in tow." And almost four fucking hours away.

"Okay."

I pulled back, jaw clenched, and she dropped to her knees without a word, following Devon into the darkness beyond. A light flickered on inside as I bent to shut them in.

"Come back for us," Mila whispered.

"Only the devil himself would keep me from you."

Tears glistened in her eyes, and I shut the door, leaving my emotions, my humanity inside with her.

If those trucks carried anyone but friends, the night wouldn't end pretty.

I slipped outside into the night, a quick glance down the lane showing it dark as midnight. A quick call through to Stone gave me the answers I needed.

The trucks had stopped at the halfway point and six guys approached on foot.

I shot off a text to Ryker.

Bring up the cleaners. We're about to make a mess.

I turned off my ringer and made myself comfortable beside the firewood stack where I had a clear view of the driveway and open area in the middle of the bunk houses.

Stone was best with hand to hand combat as a black belt, so he, too, stayed on the ground and close by.

Hammer and Crow had both been in the military—one sharpshooter and the other a spotter. They would have gotten set atop their bunk house, but I couldn't see jack shit in the darkness.

Our campfire had burned to glowing embers in the meadow's center, but it gave off little light. The towering trees kept whatever moon tried to peek from the clouds from sight, but Stone had come prepared.

I pulled the goggles over my eyes, and the place lit up in a green eerie light. Sin and Greed hid closest to where the driveway met the parking area, but Hammer had us all covered. Not that I expected the fuckers to come walking up the drive for a friendly neighborhood chat.

I shoved the ear piece Stone had provided into my ear, my head swiveling side to side, watching for any hint of movement. A quick flick of the button put me live.

"Devil," I whispered, knowing Stone would have already gotten him patched through and ready to be our eyes in the darkness. "Give me something—I don't want to just start shooting if it's some kids looking for a place to party."

"It's him. Harlon," Devil's voice came through loud and clear.

"You're sure?"

"The swastika on his left cheek is kinda hard to mistake."

Fuck. How the fuck had he found us?

"How far out?"

"Two hundred yards."

Knowing all my brothers on site were listening in, I slowed my breathing, thankful as fuck for my IT geek brother.

"Two splitting off to the west," Devil murmured in my ear.

I caught sight of Stone slipping through the shadows, heading their way.

"Two heading east."

I couldn't see a flash of movement, but trusted Greed to do as planned if any fuckers thought to surround us.

"The final two—Harlon on the left—just inside the woods but approaching along the driveway."

Radio silence fell.

A near silent pop sounded a few minutes later, followed by a grunt, and I strained my ears, my breathing too fucking loud, my muscles tensed to explode.

"Harlon's mine," I whispered what I'd already told my brothers a few times.

The fucker thought he could show up and exact revenge on the best thing he'd ever had? Cock-sucking prick had another think coming.

I set aside the rifle and pulled out my Glock. If it came to shots, then so be it, but I hoped to hell to get my fists on the fucker before he went down.

"He's mine," I whispered again, hoping like fuck Hammer would let the fucker through.

30

MILA

We sat hunkered together in stifling silence, Devon pressed tight against my side, my arm around him, and his head on my shoulder. He smelled like a pubescent boy in need of a shower coated by campfire smoke, but I drank his warmth and the scent of my son in, knowing it could very well be our last minutes together.

My heart fractured at being separated from Vigil, but I didn't question the need for us to be shut away. With us out of sight, in relative safety, he would be able to focus. Do what needed done.

I wondered what that might be, even though deep inside my gut I already knew. If Harlan and his men approached, blood would be shed.

Eyes closed, I told myself it was necessary, that

the law had failed as it often did to protect those in need.

"He'll keep us safe, Mom."

"I know," I said on automatic, not really giving my words much thought.

"No. Really." His tone held a finality beyond mere hope.

I opened my eyes and pulled back so Devon lifted his head off my shoulder. "Are you privy to something I'm not?"

He studied me for a few seconds, lips pursed, before drawing a breath deep into his lungs. "Vigil and his brothers know how to protect their loved ones."

"You're talking like you've seen it."

"He told me." Devon glanced at the secret door against the far wall.

"Told you what?"

"You can't hate him, Mom."

My insides stilled. "What did he do, Dev?"

Devon studied his hands and licked his lips. "Their father beat up their mom all the time. Cops didn't do jack shit."

I let the curse slide.

"He killed her." Devon looked up at me, and I kept my face neutral, all-too familiar with how easy it was to end a life with fists. I'd lost my and Harlon's baby—and almost my own.

"Go on," I whispered.

"Vigil and Ricky took the law into their own hands."

"They killed their father."

Devon stared me down for a full minute before nodding.

I let his words sift through my head. My heart. Vigil had trusted my son with a dark secret, and I had no question as to why. He'd proved to Devon he would go to the ends of the earth to protect his own —that was why Devon trusted him without question.

But Vigil had to know that sort of violence went against everything I wanted for my son. He had to have known I would turn my back on his offer of friendship if I found out his secret.

My son's trust was more important than his fear of losing both of us.

Tears clogged my throat, and I tugged Devon close again.

"He's a good man, Mom."

I smiled as a tear slid down my cheek. "I know."

"Will you let him make you his old lady?"

The thought thrilled me as much as it scared me.

"You got a second chance at love," Devon continued, his voice insistent. "You better take it."

"If we get out of here alive..." My throat swelled and I kissed the top of his head. "If he gets out of this alive, I will."

We sat in silence, my stomach churning, shoulders tight, and chest aching. I wanted to crawl out of that damn hole and find out what the hell was going on, but I was no stupid girl like in a suspense story. I knew how to do as told and stay put.

A muffled gun shot rang out, and my breath caught, ears ringing.

"Gunshot," Devon whispered, and I nodded.

Every minute seemed like an hour, but no other sounds reached us. Enough time lapsed, I swallowed against rising nausea, knowing Vigil should have gotten back to us if he'd been able to.

"What should we do, Mom?" My son sounded like a little boy, and I hugged him tighter, offering him assurance I didn't feel.

"Stay put, Dev. We gotta stay put."

31

VIGIL

The lone fucker approached like a wraith in the night, black on black, slinking from shadow to shadow as an owl hooted through the stillness. Whoever had snuck along with him didn't show. Not that I'd expected to, knowing how Hammer could shoot.

An unmuffled shot sounded to my left—Greed or Sin—and the thumps of fists hitting flesh followed. One shout. Two more gun shots.

I watched Harlon pause behind my truck and waited for my ear piece to crackle to life.

"Both east men down," Sin whispered, and I knew they would circle around the back toward where Stone was set to clash with two of his own.

No sound rose from the west, but Stone didn't

bother keeping his voice down when he said, "These two fuckers are already down."

"The fucker in my sites is on his own," Hammer whispered.

"He's mine." I stood and walked into the open, gun held out at the ready, my focus on Harlon. He held a gun at his side and hadn't yet seen me. "Flanders!"

He jerked sideways a good two feet—and I knew he saw me through the darkness by the way his head steadied in my direction.

"Bring your ass out here in the open," I called out, wanting to pop one in his forehead but wanting to smash in his face even more. "All five of your men are down—for fucking *good*. Payback for eight years ago you mother fucking cunt!"

He let out a roar and charged, gun tossed to the side, and I grinned.

Bring it.

I dropped my gun, tore off the goggles and met him halfway, a grunt ripping from me as we collided by the fire pit.

"Where's my wife?" he growled as we both landed punches.

"Ex, you fucker." I smashed my fist against his jaw, and he went down—with me on top of him.

He got in a couple hits, but he was no match for the cold focus I held onto. Every crunch against his face earned me one less punch to my side. Every splatter of his blood against my front and beard one less buck of his hips beneath me trying to break free.

The camp's flood lights kicked on, but I didn't let up until he stilled beneath me, wheezing for breath through his busted mouth and what was left of his nose. I wanted to drag out the fight for another couple of hours, peeling the skin from his body in slow agony for every minute he'd hurt Mila.

But my woman and Devon had been in that basement long enough as it was. Time to get answers and put an end to shit.

"How'd you know where to find us?" I hissed, inches from his face.

"Fuck. You." He spit in my face, and I sat back, smashing him in the cheek, the bones already fucking shattered. He groaned, and I asked again.

Of course, he didn't answer.

Another fist to the face, another groan. I'd already given thought to how he could have found out, and I knew for fact not a single Viper brother would have revealed where we'd gone.

"Was it Pritt?" I asked, leaning down again, needing to see the one eye I hadn't yet swelled shut.

He closed his eye and wheezed.

I pulled my knife from the sheath inside my boot and stabbed him through the shoulder.

"Ah!" He shrieked and bowed beneath me.

"Talk, mother fucker," I said through grit teeth.

Harlon sputtered and spit but didn't say a word.

I ground my knife around a bit, digging into bone and smiling as the stench of piss rose from beneath me. "Pansy assed little bitch. Tell me, and I'll end it quick."

"Fuck you."

I yanked out my blade, flipped it to my left hand, and sank it into his other shoulder, his screams like fucking music to my ears. "I can go all night long, Harlon. All of your men are dead, and we're out here in the middle of fucking nowhere. Might as well spill the truth or I'm gonna take my good old time spilling your guts."

"Pritt." He gasped as I yanked my blade free. "Stacy Pritt."

Mother fucking cunt.

I swept my blade over Harlon's throat and watched him choke on his own blood until his mouth stopped working and one good eye went blank.

A few heaved breaths left me before I finally

lifted my head. My brothers stood around me in a ring, all staring, not a single one with a trace of remorse or disgust in their eyes. I shoved my knife back in the sheath.

"Devil?" I asked into my mic.

"Already on Pritt," Devil replied, and I let out a rushed exhale, knowing I wouldn't have to worry about that fucker.

"Vigil?" Stone asked, his face and chest splattered with blood.

"I'm good." I stood, flexing my hands. "Toss their bodies in the trucks and put them in the old barn out back. I already told Ryker to bring up the cleaners, but get this shit cleaned up the best you can."

I stalked toward the house, every inch of my skin crackling with energy, the fire inside of me still burning bright.

"Vigil."

I turned to find Sin jogging to catch up to me, pulling his t-shirt off overhead.

"Might want to at least wipe off your face first." He tossed me his shirt, and I nodded my thanks before continuing on my way, doing as he'd suggested.

I yanked that damn clothes basket away and pulled open the hatch with shaking hands.

Bright light hit me in the face, and I raised a hand to shield my face. "It's me. It's okay."

"Oh God..." Mila whispered as I backed out of her way, and she got a good look at me. She stood and threw her arms around me regardless of the blood, and the tension drained out of me.

Devon scrambled up and eyed me, his dark eyes round as they landed on my face and flitted down over my splattered clothing.

I stuck out my free arm, and he smashed into me, his hands clutching at my sweatshirt same as his mom's.

"Harlon?" Mila whispered against my chest.

"No longer a concern," I said, fighting off the adrenaline crash shakes. "I told you I would keep you safe. No one is going to touch what's mine."

Devon chuckled amidst the gore and obvious violence. "Told you, Mom."

A shuddered sigh went through Mila, and I hugged them both tighter, my eyes closing in a prayer of thankfulness to a God I normally didn't give two shits about.

32

MILA

Hours later, I finally got Vigil to lay down in bed with me. He hadn't allowed me or Devon outside even after Ryker and a handful of other brothers showed up to deal with the mess. Vigil had showered, handed off his bloodied clothes, and then got on his cell with Devil. I heard enough to know that Marshal Pritt had been the inside man who'd led Harlon to us.

I also heard the news that Stacy Pritt had breathed his last breath and he would soon be swimming with the fishes.

"Why'd he do it?" I asked, knowing like me, that Vigil couldn't sleep even though it was after four in the morning.

"His father always had it out for Ricky and me."

Vigil snapped his mouth shut, his entire body going tense.

I nuzzled my cheek against his chest, and snuggled closer against his side, entwining my legs between his. "Devon told me about what you and your brother did."

A rushed exhale left his lips, fluttering my bangs on my forehead. "And you're still here."

"There's no other place I'd rather be, Vigil." I propped up onto an elbow to find his blue-gray eyes intently studying me in the bathroom light we'd left on.

He pushed my hair back from my face, and I leaned into his palm. "I'm not a good man."

I couldn't keep from smirking. "Devon seems to think you are." My smile faded as his face remained stern. "We all have demons," I whispered, tracing his lower lip with my fingertip. "But you've slayed yours —and mine. That makes you pretty damn good in my book, Frankie Capello."

He grimaced. "Call me Vigil."

I smiled again, but my lips flatlined when he didn't respond. "Those high school boys?"

A shadow flitted over his face, but he held my steady gaze. "Wasn't my hand, but it was on my orders. Not gonna lie, wildcat. Those boys picking on your son also gang-raped a girl last year and got her pregnant. A botched abortion came after dozens of pay offs. Those boys got away with what no man should."

"Is she okay?" I asked, my stomach in knots as demons tried to raise their ugly heads from the memories in my mind.

"She will be—eventually."

I nodded, digesting yet another mouthful of words and truth. "Is everything going to be okay for us?"

"It will." His voice held conviction. "Two other Demons got loose during the transit, but my Viper brothers in Vegas are taking care of that little problem. There's a dozen still behind bars, but their days are numbered as well. It's time to end them once and for all."

Knowing what I did about the Demons' club—the abuse and rape of women, the running of guns and drugs, never mind the young girls who'd disappeared from our neighborhoods without a trace...

"I'm glad," I whispered, closing my eyes once more. "I trust you, Vigil."

He squeezed me tight, and I gave into exhaustion.

I woke to Vigil rolling me onto my back, settling his hard, hot body between my thighs. "Morning, wildcat."

I blinked in the bright sunlight shining through the windows to find a wary face peering down at me. "Morning," I said with a soft smile, running my palm along his whiskered cheek, shifting my hips to rub his hard length along my clit.

His pale eyes lightened as though my simple greeting lifted tension clear off his body. Vigil might be a brutal beast of a man, but he was so much more.

"Look at me like that," he muttered with a glint in his eye while rocking against me, "and I might beg you to ink my claim on your fine as fuck body."

"Look at *me* like that, and I'll drag your ass to the tattoo shop myself."

Vigil took my hands and pressed them overhead. My legs wrapped around his waist without thought, and he pushed slowly into my body, our gazes locked, and our hearts thrumming between us.

"You gonna let me love you forever, Mila Zeigler?"

"Only if you'll let me love you back."

He bottomed out, but held still, his cock twitching deep inside me. "You gonna let me adopt that son of yours?"

"If he'll have you—and you promise to love him, too."

Vigil's smirk caught my breath, and he leaned in to swipe his lips over mine. "It's a deal, wildcat."

THE END

———

ABOUT THE AUTHOR

Lynn Burke is a full-time mother, voracious gardener, and International Bestselling Author of hot romance books. A country bumpkin turned Bay Stater, she enjoys her chowdah and Dunkin Donuts when not trying to escape the reality of city life.

ALSO BY LYNN BURKE

Blood Born Series

Bonds of Worship Series

Darkest Desires Series

Dark Leopards MC

Devil's Outlaws MC

Elite Escort Series

Fallen Gliders MC

Found by Fate Series

Midnight Sun Series

Missing Link Series

Risso Family Series

Sandy Ridge Series

Vicious Vipers MC

Standalone Titles:

Abel's Obsession

Divulging Secrets

Healing Storms

In Between

The Playboy Bachelor